Wednesday's Child

Clare Revell

Wednesday's Child

Contact Information: titleadmin@pelicanbookgroup.com

Cover Art by Nicola Martinez

White Rose Publishing, a division of Pelican Ventures, LLC
www.pelicanbookgroup.com PO Box 1738 *Aztec, NM * 87410

White Rose Publishing Circle and Rosebud logo is a trademark of Pelican Ventures, LLC

Publishing History
First White Rose Edition, 2013
Print Edition ISBN 978-1-61116-214-1
Electronic Edition ISBN 978-1-61116-213-4
Published in the United States of America

Monday's Child must hide for protection
Tuesday's Child tenders direction
Wednesday's Child grieves for his soul
Thursday's Child chases the whole
Friday's Child is a man obsessed
Saturday's Child might be possessed
And Sunday's Child on life's seas is tossed
Awaiting the Lifeboat that rescues the lost

Dedication

To Nanny

Other titles by Clare Revell

Novels
After the Fire
Monday's Child
Tuesday's Child

Novellas
Season for Miracles
Cassie's Wedding Dress
Time's Arrow

Dollar Downloads
Saving Christmas

Free Reads
Kisses from Heaven

Praise for Clare Revell

Monday's Child
Packed with action and laced with faith, this romance builds excitement for the next book in the series of seven romantic suspense novels based on a rewrite of the popular nursery rhyme, Monday's Child. ~ Author, Dora Hiers

Times Arrow
I stand in awe of Revell's ability to pack an entire novel's worth of action and emotion into so few pages. ~ Author, Delia Latham

After The Fire
What a wild ride in *After the Fire*! Ms. Revell created a sweet romance within a beautiful setting, but don't let that fool you. There's plenty of action in this book as Freddie and Jason work to uncover the truth. Just when you think you're near 'The End,'   Ms. Revell pulls out a few more surprises. ~ Author, Dora Hiers

Glossary

Li — pronounced Lie. Liam's nickname
Niamh — pronounced Neeve. Liam's twin sister
Ni — pronounced Nigh — Niamh's nickname
Pi — pronounced Pie — Patrick's nickname. Also known as three point one four. Patrick is Liam's older brother.
CPS — Crown Prosecution Service
Mke — Swahili for wife
Mkewe — Swahili for his wife

1

Wednesday's child grieves for his soul...

'For I know the plans I have for you,' declares the Lord, 'plans to prosper you and not to harm you, plans to give you hope and a future. Then you will call upon me and come and pray to me and I will listen to you. You will seek me and find me when you seek me with all your heart.' Jeremiah 29:11-13

Matumaini Mission, Endarra, Africa

The melodic rise and fall of thirty children's voices raised in worship drew Liam from his desk to the doorway of the mission office. He gazed over the sandy compound already shimmering under the intense blaze of the sun, and it was still two hours before noon.

On the steps of the school house, his wife of three years, Sally, sang with the orphaned children, her clear soprano leading the way, her hands guiding them with the actions. "The rains came down and the floods went whoosh, and the house on the sand fell flat, like that."

Liam laughed as, at the last two words, all the children, whether they were four, sixteen, or somewhere in between, fell to the ground in unison. Without this mission, these children would be on the streets, the boys press-ganged into the local militia, a much worse fate awaited the girls, with very few of them surviving into adulthood.

The name of the mission was *Matumaini* which was Swahili for hope. And with God's grace, that is what all these children now had. They'd leave here educated and, God willing, with a faith that would last until they were called Home.

Sally sat on the steps, explaining the story behind the song they'd just sung. Once she finished, he'd take them inside the relatively cool building for their next lesson. This was only the second week he and Sally had been here. Sent from Headley Cross Baptist on a short term mission, now neither of them could imagine ever doing anything else. Once they got home next month, they'd look into doing this permanently.

Happy and content to serve God this way, they'd agreed to put off having a family of their own for a couple more years. Sally would make such a good mother. But right now she was a surrogate mother to a whole load of children who needed her. And she excelled at it. He hadn't seen her happier since the day he married her.

A truck engine caught his attention and Liam turned towards the gate. They weren't expecting anyone and the supply truck didn't come until tomorrow. As he took the three steps down to the sand, the truck accelerated, bursting through the gate with a crash, a screech of metal and chink of chain.

In a heart-stopping instant, the joy vanished.

Blood pounded in his ears. A stomach churning realization gripped him. His breath caught in his throat as four heavily armed men leapt to the ground, the instant the truck swerved to a halt in a cloud of sand.

Gunfire filled the air. The children leapt to their feet, screaming, panic-stricken.

Sally ran down the steps, putting herself between

the children and the gunmen, ordering the youngsters to run inside and hide.

Liam began sprinting across the compound, desperate to get to his wife. "Sally…"

She turned, just as a hail of bullets caught her body. She staggered and fell, the force of the gunfire twisting her around.

"Nooooo…." Liam ran faster. A bullet ripped into his shoulder and he cried out, falling to the ground. Another shattered his knee. Pain ricocheted through him. He started to crawl across the compound, sand filling his seared lungs. Every breath he took was a gasp of effort. Every movement sent shards of agony through his battered body.

God, please, help us. Let someone get to the armory and protect us. Let me reach Sally. God, defend us against these men. You are all powerful, overrule here. Stop the assault. Save us.

Around him, the sound of gunfire mingled with deafening explosions. Another bullet tore into him, knocking him to the ground again. He laid there, blood streaming from his face, more pain slicing through him. Darkness rushed towards him like a freight train and slammed into him, sounds fading, as it carried him away with great speed.

When he opened his eyes, the truck was gone. Crackling and roaring filled his ears and an orange glow lit the compound. Thick black smoke belched from the buildings, mushrooming into the blue sky. Bodies of the children and other missionaries lay around him. He had to get to Sally. Her hand stretched towards him, eyes beseeching him to do something. He tried to stand and fell back to the ground his knee exploding in pain. Ignoring the agony from his torn shoulder, he pulled his way across the sand towards her. It seemed to take forever before he finally gathered her into his arms.

Please, God, don't let her die.

He wanted to speak, to tell her he loved her and not to leave him, but he couldn't. His jaw wouldn't work. Blood dripped off his face onto her shirt.

Sally whimpered in his arms and her grip on him loosened. Her head fell to one side.

Smoke and flames rose high into the air.

Please God, I'm begging You, don't do this. Let me wake up. Please God, let me wake and find this has all been a dream. If You love me at all, don't do this...

He looked down at his wife. Tears ran unabated down his face before he finally gave into the consuming blackness, falling face down across her lifeless body.

1

Eighteen months later

Liam Page placed his lunch order in the café and then glanced at the clock on the wall. Where had his lunch hour gone? Twenty minutes to eat this before he was due back. A sure fire way to guarantee heartburn if ever there was one. He should've stuck to 'plan A' and eaten lunch at work. Or at least gone home to pick up his lunch from where it still sat on the counter by the kettle where he'd left it. 'Plan B' would have worked if there wasn't a ten-mile queue in the bakers. 'Plan C' failed as the supermarket was out of sandwiches, and he refused to pay almost four quid for a tiny salad. So, here he was, stuck with 'Plan D'.

"Thank you." Liam smiled at the assistant and paid for his food. He picked up the tray and glanced around the small café. There was only one free table. Wedged into a corner, almost like an afterthought, getting to it was a juggling act in itself. Maybe he was in the wrong profession. He should quit teaching and run away to join the circus. He set the tray down and squeezed himself into the space between the chair and table.

On second thoughts he should just skip lunch in future—or stick to the salad. He could do with losing a few pounds off his waistline if a "normal" person should fit in here. Liam allowed himself a wry smile as he looked down at the sausage, eggs and chips. He'd start the diet tomorrow. He wasn't overweight, but perhaps it wouldn't hurt to keep in shape a little more than he did. Not that he had anyone to nag him about his diet now. A home cooked meal consisted of something that came out of the freezer and into the microwave and eaten alone in front of the television. He covered the chips with vinegar and salt and added a dollop of ketchup before wolfing it down.

That, he decided a little too late, was definitely a bad idea. The first pangs of indigestion assailed him. He'd probably be cranky for the rest of the day. Would the kids notice? Probably not. They said he was cranky all the time, anyway. It did have its advantages…as silence fell whenever he walked down the corridor. However his reputation as one of the fairest members of staff stood him in good stead and the kids knew he had their backs whenever they needed help.

Liam picked up his tea and glanced at the woman at the next table, laptop and papers spread in front of her. His gaze settled on her for a proper look, taking in every aspect. She was a stunner. As a child he and his twin used to guess people's occupations from the way they dressed, not that they'd often found out if they were right. With long, dark hair reaching half way down her back, and a smart green blouse tucked into a black plaid skirt, the woman looked like a lawyer. Years ago, he would have found the time to at least say hello, but that was before…

His eyes blurred for a moment as he saw Sally in his mind's eye—her long hair flowing behind her as he pushed her on the swing, the echo of her laughter hanging on the breeze. He shook his head to clear the thought and ran his fingers over the plain gold band on his left hand. Those days were long gone.

Liam wiped his mouth on the serviette and stood. Wearing his lunch wasn't part of the professional image he needed to project. A glance at his watch showed he had ten minutes to get back. Time, tide, and a class of thirty kids at Headley Cross Secondary School waited for no one. He could hardly chastise the kids about being late for class if he was guilty of the same offence himself, could he?

He began to edge out of the space which now seemed smaller than before, and bumped his hip on the table behind him.

"Hey, watch where you're going."

"Sorry." Liam turned around, hitting the table again. He watched in horror as the table shifted, like a view in slow motion. The vase of flowers tipped over, sending water all over the laptop and papers.

"Oh no! That's all I need." The female voice, as soft and silky as he imagined, was tinged with dismay and anger.

His face flaming, Liam snatched a pile of napkins from her side. "I'm so sorry. Let me help."

"I think you've done enough." Irritation flashed in her hazel eyes as she glared at him. "Just leave it. I'll do it." She picked up the flowers and shoved them back into the vase.

Liam's cheeks burned, matching the churning in his stomach as it rebelled against his lunch. Dumping the napkins on the table, he pulled a pen from his jacket and scrawled his number on one of them. "I'll pay for any repairs your computer needs. My name's Liam Page. This is my mobile number. The phone's on all the time. If you get voice mail, just leave a message,

Miss...?"

The woman flinched as she took it, her cool fingers sending waves of heat through him as they brushed his hand. "Miss Dorne. No doubt I'll be in touch"—she glanced down—"Mr. Page."

Liam took a deep breath, wanting to say more, but not sure what to say. His apology wasn't enough, so what else was there? "I'm very sorry. If there's anything I can do—"

Her cold voice cut him off. "I have your number."

He took a deep breath and made a hasty exit, now later than ever. Glancing back, he could still see Miss Dorne sitting, staring at the mess he'd created. It looked like despair on her face, but he wasn't sure. He hesitated. Should he go back in and help clean it up? He ought to but he'd made enough of a scene, and she'd been quite emphatic about wanting him to leave. She rubbed her face. Was she crying? Deciding in this case that discretion was the better part of valor, Liam turned away. He never had liked seeing a woman cry. There was something about a woman's tears that rocked him to the core.

Part of him hoped she would call him about her computer. At least he'd speak to her again. She had captured his interest like no woman had since before he'd met Sally. But then maybe it'd be better if she didn't call.

The repair bill would no doubt use a sizeable chunk of the money he had saved for his trip to Endarra in the summer. As well as the flights and hotel, he'd need travel money for cabs and other things.

The reason behind the trip was simple. He intended to hunt down the people responsible for the murder of his wife and see that justice was done.

Liam reached the school and punched in the code. The gates swung open. Since the Dunblane shootings, school security was tight. Not even parents could get into the building without permission or a prior appointment.

He dodged the children streaming across the car park and front quad and entered reception. Signing in, Liam smiled at the prefects carrying the registers to the form rooms and headed to the gents. He stood at the sink and splashed cold water on his face for a moment, his mind's eye still seeing her at the table.

You're an idiot. After ruining her laptop, you didn't even get her number. Shaking his head, Liam dried off and pulled the tie from his pocket. He buttoned his shirt, and knotted the tie before heading into the corridor to find the classroom where his class of fourteen year olds should be lined up by the door, waiting for their English lesson. Hopefully poetry analysis would keep the image of the attractive Miss Dorne out of his mind.

****

The café door swung shut. Jacqui shook her head as she gazed in dismay at the soggy sheets of paper and the equally soggy laptop with its blank screen. Water trickled from the casing, pooling onto the table beneath it.

Tears burned her eyes and she blinked hard. She put so much time and effort into this presentation, and now, thanks to the tall Irish stranger and a vase of long stemmed yellow, green, and white carnations it was ruined. Grabbing the napkins the man had left, she blotted the mess, praying as she did so.

Oh, Lord, what do I do now? I've got two hours before the meeting. That's nowhere near long enough to redo everything—even if I did have time to get back to the office. Lord, there is so much riding on this. It's my chance to prove both to the boss and myself that I can do this. Oh please, forgive me.

I hope I wasn't too rude to him, even if he did deserve it. She pulled herself up short. No one deserved any degree of rudeness, no matter what they'd done. Even if they had ruined both five weeks work *and* her laptop in one foul swoop.

Jacqui closed her eyes, seeing him again in her mind's eye. His tight white shirt, with the three buttons undone, didn't do a very good job hiding the perfect abs and broad shoulders beneath it. And his slacks emphasized a trim waist and hips. Never mind the intoxicating waft of cologne she detected as he leaned over her. He had a thick silver chain around his left wrist, peeking from under his shirt sleeve. And he was handsome...she'd never found beards particularly attractive on a man, but his...

She shook her head and massaged her temples. All men were the same and she didn't want or need another one in her life. *That's enough. Think of something else, like how to fix the mess you are in right now.*

There was a backup file on the office computer—but she didn't have time to drive all the way into Wokingham and back again. If someone could bring her that and a spare laptop she could still run her presentation. Jacqui pulled her phone from her bag. At least that hadn't been on the table during the flood. She dialed the office, hoping someone would be there.

Relief flooded her as the phone clicked. "Jekyll

Foundation, Eve Myers speaking."

"Hey, Eve, it's Jacqui. Sorry to bother you, but I had a slight accident with the presentation."

"What happened? Are you all right?"

"I made the mistake of stopping for lunch and had it on the table for a final check. Some bloke spilled water over the laptop and the papers. The laptop's fried, no make that drowned as there's water dripping from it, and the papers soaked. I don't suppose you have time to bring a spare over?"

"No, but for you I'll make an exception."

Jacqui smiled. *Thank You, Lord, for friends like Eve.* "Thank you. I could hug you. The folder containing the files I need is on my office computer. It's called Head Sec. I'll have to find a printer here for more printouts, but…"

"Rubbish. Even if you find a local printer, it will cost you a fortune at five pence a sheet. It won't take long for me to print more off. How many copies do you need?"

Sucking in a deep breath, Jacqui did a quick mental count. "Twenty should do it. It's a three page document called Head Sec dot doc. It should be in the same folder. Are you sure?"

"Don't argue or I might change my mind. Where are you?"

"Headley Cross. Where else would I be?" She glanced up as the café manager appeared with a pile of tea towels and cloths. "Thank you."

The manager knelt and dealt with the floor.

"You know what I mean," her friend chided. "Headley Cross may be small, but it's a town of over two thousand people. Where in Headley Cross?" Eve's voice was no longer tinged with concern. It was full on mother-hen mode. Just what she didn't need.

People moved and chatted around her. Cutlery chinked and conversations rose and fell. Grateful she was no longer the center of attention, Jacqui grabbed another tea towel. "Right now I'm clearing up the mess he made. He offered to help, but I didn't want him to. By the time you get here, I'll be sitting outside Coronation Hall. It's on the main road behind the precinct. You can also park for free for twenty minutes there."

"Cool—my kind of car park. All right, it's printing and collating, now. Give me thirty minutes at the most and I'll be there."

"Thanks, Eve. You're a life saver." Jacqui hung up and put away her phone. She looked at the manager. "I am so sorry about this."

"Its fine, not your fault as we saw what happened. Do you want another meal to replace that one?"

She paused to look at her plate. Her cheese and tomato sandwich was swimming in a sea of water. A broken yellow carnation sat on top like some kind of crown. "No, thank you."

"Let me at least get you a refund. I insist."

Not wanting a refund, but wanting a fuss even less, Jacqui agreed. "OK, thank you."

As he vanished behind the counter, she cleared up the rest of the mess. Scrunching up the napkins, she tossed them onto her plate. Folding the sodden papers, she left them on the plate as well. She shut the defunct laptop and not wanting to ruin its case as well, tucked it under her arm. She headed outside into the sunshine, without waiting for the manager to return with her refund.

A landscape architect working for the Jekyll

Foundation, Jacqui couldn't afford to lose this tender. She wouldn't go as far as to say her whole career hinged on it, but it was the first time the Foundation had trusted her to prepare and present a proposal on her own.

Crossing the courtyard, she found a huge, twisted oak tree that provided shelter from the sun. Her favorite of all trees, it set her imagination ablaze with thoughts of all the ancient gnarled oak had seen in its long life. Battles, lover's trysts, maybe even royalty passing. When this magnificent tree was a sapling, Henry VIII was king.

She pulled a band from her pocket and twisted her hair up in a ponytail. She hadn't expected the day to turn out so hot. Most unusual for England, they were having a spring heat wave, bringing the ducklings and flowers out early.

A raised circular bed of yellow daffodils interspersed with red and orange tulips waved in the breeze. Bluebells filled the grass as far as her eyes could see and by her feet, yellow primroses and white snowdrops peeked through the earth around the base of the tree. No matter how good she or the others were at mixing flowers and colors, God always did it so much better.

A family of swans and cygnets glided along the tranquil water under the bridge. Her fingers smoothed over the gold cross around her neck, the last gift from her parents. She never took it off, clinging to the final link with them. Her gaze followed the swans. Family was something she didn't have. Although she dreamed about meeting the perfect man, she didn't expect to find him any time soon.

Her mind went back to the guy who knocked over

the flowers. Hopefully the laptop was going to be all right. She didn't want to have any more contact with this Mr. Page than was absolutely necessary, no matter how attractive he was. Flipping up the laptop, and hoping she wouldn't get electrocuted, she tried starting it again.

Nothing. It wouldn't even boot up. The black screen stared mockingly at her. Her lap got damper. She sighed. She wished she could have asked for a change of clothes as well. She zipped the laptop into the case, forgetting about saving the case. It would dry out a lot easier than the computer and her clothes needed to dry.

"Hey." The voice of her colleague cut through her thoughts.

Jacqui looked up and managed a faint smile as Eve plumped down on the bench beside her. "Hi, Eve."

"You look like the world just ended, or you lost a shilling and found a penny."

"My grandmother used to say that. But it may as well have."

"So what happened? Other than some guy spilling his water all over your work, that is."

"Actually, it wasn't his water. It was a whole vase of flowers."

"I've heard of 'say it with flowers', but that's ridiculous."

Jacqui scowled. "To add insult to injury, the carnations were dyed green, and you know how much I hate florists faking the color in flowers, by soaking them in food coloring. But as far as the laptop is concerned, it won't even boot up no matter how much I try. I'm sorry."

Eve held up another case. "No problem. It's hardly

your fault. I brought another. I loaded your files on it, plus put a USB pen in as back up. I also put thirty copies of your print outs in there. I know you said twenty, but figured a few extra wouldn't hurt."

Jacqui smiled and swapped the case for one containing the damaged computer. "Thank you so much. I owe you."

"You can bring doughnuts to work for coffee break for the rest of the week." Eve crossed one leg over the other. "So, what's he like? This mystery man who's got you all worked up and hot under the collar."

Jacqui took a deep breath. "He's tall, has dark hair, a beard, brown eyes, and an Irish accent. He looks a bit like a movie star and scores an eight on the hunk rating."

Her friend snorted. "You managed to take all that in as he knocked a vase of carnations on your laptop? You got it bad, girl."

Jacqui pulled a face. She wasn't in the mood for teasing. "The guy left me his name and number and offered to pay to get the computer fixed."

"Did he? That was good of him. It may be fine once it's dried out. You never know your luck."

"I don't do luck."

"This time you may need it. I'll get the I.T. guy to take a look at it this afternoon. If you give me his card, I can ring this guy if we need it fixed."

"Sure I have it somewhere. Uh..." Jacqui fumbled for the napkin in her pockets, and then closed her eyes. "It was on a serviette. I must have used it to mop up the water. How stupid can I get?" She pushed her hands though her hair in frustration. "They better be able to fix it. I don't want to have to pay for it, especially now I've lost his number."

"Can you remember his name?"

Jacqui scrunched her nose up as she tried to think. "Page...Liam Page. I think he said. I wasn't paying much attention," she said, after a few seconds.

Eve's eyebrows vanished into her fringe in amazement. She tilted her head, waving her foot. "You remember exactly what he looks like, right down to his accent, but you weren't paying much attention to his name...interesting."

"Eve, please, drop it. He's a man and I'm off men."

"For now. It's probably best not to swear off men for life, though. They do have their uses."

"You know very well what Vince did to me. I have no wish to get involved with any man, thank you. And don't tell me all men aren't the same. I can't relax enough around any of them. Not even the boss. I flinch every time he leans across my desk or gets into my personal space."

Eve raised a hand in self-defense. "OK, OK, subject dropped. You're right. I'm sorry. Let's just see what I.T. says before you panic over the laptop, and *possibly* contacting this Mr. Page."

"All right." She tapped the case. "Thanks for bringing this over."

Eve got up, taking the dead laptop with her. "You're welcome. I've got to get back to the office." She shook a finger at Jacqui and winked. "No more flowers. Especially ones thrown at you by Irish hunks."

Jacqui managed a small laugh. She'd rather go to the dentist and that was saying something. "I promise."

****

The bell rang signifying the end of the school day. Liam glanced up at the scraping of chairs and slamming of books. "Did I say dismissed?" He shook his head at the collective sigh from his class. He taught the whole school, and it didn't matter if they were eleven or eighteen, the lesson was over and forgotten as soon as the bell rang.

He tapped his fingers on the desk and waited until they all sat down again. Their uniforms were slightly awry by the end of the day, blue shirts untucked, navy blazers tossed carelessly over the backs of the chairs and their blue and white striped ties at varying lengths.

He cast a stern look over them. "Remember the assignment on Romeo and Juliet is due in first period Monday. There will be detentions if you don't hand it in on time." He ignored the groans. "And before you ask or try it on Monday, I will not be accepting excuses such as 'my homework fell in the bath, sir' or 'the cat threw up over it, sir'. You've had a week do it." Liam uttered the words the students were longing for. "All right, now you're dismissed."

The students scrambled for the door as Liam ran his hand over his chin. The beard was an experiment, but one he'd probably end up keeping. He wasn't used to the scratchy facial hair, but it was better than seeing the scar his clothes didn't hide in the mirror each day. Besides, he hated shaving with a passion.

Pushing to his feet, he turned to the board and picked up the blackboard duster. These things hadn't changed since he and his twin sister, Niamh, were at school over two decades ago. Erasing the lesson plan, his thoughts returned to the fool he'd made of himself over lunch. He couldn't have done it better if he'd tried. Niamh would find it hysterically funny, which was one reason he wasn't going to tell her about it.

He tapped the duster and then set it on the shelf by the board. Gathering the pile of essays from his desk, he walked to the door, turned off the lights, and headed to the staff room.

He dumped the essays on a chair, and loosened his tie, wishing he could take it off. He checked his phone. No messages or calls. *Was that a good thing or not?* He'd had the image of the woman in his mind ever since lunch. His mother had told him flowers were a good way to impress a woman. But he didn't think it was the kind of impression his mother had in mind.

Liam walked over to the urn, poured his coffee and added milk. He sipped it and made his way over to the window, staring out over the bland playground filled with pupils making their way home, laughing and chatting. After today's fiasco, that's all he wanted to do. He debated playing hooky from the department head meeting with headmaster, Justin Forbes. As much as the school grounds needed something doing to them, he really didn't want to attend tonight. He sipped his coffee, his eye catching the chunky chain-link bracelet on his wrist. Sally had given it to him as a wedding present.

Liam closed his eyes and the images which haunted his nightmares filled his mind. Gunfire, blood, Sally screaming and falling...

"Liam? Are you all right? It's time for the meeting."

"Yeah, I'm fine. I'm coming."

Sliding into the single available seat, which happened to be in the front row, Liam hoped the person from the Foundation would be a quick speaker.

He honestly didn't see the point in this. Surely the decision to re-landscape the grounds was up to the governors and school body, not the department heads. He leaned back in the chair and propped the left foot on right knee. Justin stood by the desk, the woman next to him leaning over a laptop. She straightened and the short black plaid skirt gave Liam an uninterrupted view of her shapely legs.

No harm in looking, as beauty was there to be admired—whether it was a woman or the view from a mountain top. Besides, he and God parted company when Sally died, so it wasn't as if he'd come under condemnation from his conscience for it. He shook his head. What was wrong with him today? First he noticed the woman in the café at lunch and now this? Could Niamh be right about the emotional part of him that he'd thought had gone forever? Was it finally coming back to life? According to her, he'd been a robot for the past eighteen months, but part of him liked that. That way it didn't hurt quite so much.

The woman turned, giving him a glimpse of her face. The smile as she spoke to Justin lit her familiar hazel eyes.

Liam's eyes widened, no longer with appreciation, but horror. Just when he didn't think the day could get any worse. It was Miss Dorne from the café. He had to get out of here before she saw him.

He pushed upright in his chair, starting to get to his feet, then stopped. It was too late. She'd seen him.

Her eyes narrowed in recognition, and Liam took a deep breath, trying to force air into his lungs through the obstruction blocking his throat. He hoped desperately she wouldn't say anything about him ruining her computer. It must have been this presentation she was working on. She looked at Justin as he spoke, then back at Liam as they walked over to where he was seated.

Way to go, you can get fired and spend all your savings in one day.

His dread grew as the headmaster led the woman over to him. Justin smiled as he spoke. "Liam, this is Miss Jacqui Dorne. She's representing the Jekyll Foundation. Miss Dorne, this is Liam Page, head of our English department."

Liam took her cool hand in his warm one and shook it. Somehow he managed to get his voice to work and sound enthusiastic, although he felt anything but. Any hint of interest he had in this scheme had just dissipated. "It's nice to meet you, Miss Dorne. I'm looking forward to the presentation and seeing what your company has to offer."

2

Jacqui shook his hand, covering her shock at seeing him. He was the last person she'd expected to run into here. It was more than a little ironic that he'd nearly ruined the very presentation he had to watch and evaluate. "Hello, Mr. Page. I hope I live up to, that is, my company lives up to your expectations."

"It has a good reputation. I'm sure it will."

So that was the way he wanted to play it. Cool and calm. She could do that. *Be still my beating heart*. She could drown in those eyes of his. She had downplayed his attractiveness to Eve earlier. The guy oozed testosterone. Only now, he looked like a kid caught with his hand in the cookie jar. For an instant she was tempted to drop him in it. But the instant passed. She wasn't that mean. It was an accident after all, and now she'd calmed down, she knew that. At least she had the opportunity to ask for his number again.

Letting go of his hand, Jacqui sat down by the desk as Mr. Forbes started the meeting. His words flowed over her as she ran her gaze over the assembled teachers, before finally resting back on Liam Page. He was trying to look nonchalant, his legs crossed, right hand folded over his left. But there was something about him and she didn't just mean his looks.

"So, let me hand you over to Jacqui Dorne who'll tell you more."

Jacqui stood to polite applause and smiled. She'd

done this several times, but still the butterflies soared and whirled making her uncomfortable. She took a deep breath and began with a brief history of the Jekyll Foundation. "You should all have found on your seats a paper copy of our designs."

There was a rustling of papers from everyone with one exception. *It had to be him, didn't it?* Jacqui picked one up and handed it to Liam. "Here you go."

"Thank you." He reached out his left hand and took it, the gold band catching in the overhead lights. How could she have missed it before? His eyes were on her necklace as he spoke. At least she hoped he stared at her necklace. Clearing her throat made him lift his eyes back to her face, a faint smile on his lips. What kind of a game was he playing?

Staying as professional as she could, Jacqui turned back to the laptop. He was married and off limits. The good looking ones always were. Either that, or they were creeps—and she'd had her fill of them. "I'll answer any questions you may have at the end."

She started the program and sat. Watching the presentation with a critical eye, she winced over a couple of the sentences, wishing she'd phrased them differently. The borrowed laptop had an older version of the program and it had completely messed up her text. A smaller font than the one she'd spent so long choosing to compliment the pictures filled the screen, and it was much too close to the images. A couple of slides were also the wrong way around, but hopefully no one would notice the order, and it wouldn't sway them against giving her the contract.

Taking her eyes off the screen for a moment, she caught Liam watching her and quickly looked away. The presentation had finished. Jacqui closed the program and rose to her feet. "Does anyone have any questions?"

****

Liam was more than a little distracted as Miss Dorne gave her presentation, unable to take his eyes off her. He barely heard what she said, instead watching the way she moved and used her hands as she spoke. Like Sally. So much about this woman reminded him of Sally. He wasn't sure why. Sally was as fair as Miss Dorne was dark. Perhaps it was simply the cross around her neck. He'd bought Sally one as a wedding present, and she never took it off. Not even in the shower.

The following debate was short, with the majority liking the designs. The headmaster thanked Miss Dorne and dismissed everyone.

Liam stayed in his seat, watching her pack away her things. Then he unfolded his legs and stood, moving over to her. "Miss Dorne?"

Jacqui's gaze met his, pulling him into their depths. "Mr. Page. Did the presentation live up to your expectations?"

"Yes, it did. I, uh, I wanted to apologize again for earlier. Did you get the laptop working?"

"It wouldn't even boot up. I had to get a replacement from work or there would have been no presentation this afternoon. Fortunately, all the files were backed up on the Foundation servers, so my work wasn't destroyed."

"That's good. I'm glad I didn't ruin your presentation completely."

She pushed a stray hair behind her ear. "Only the

laptop."

Liam's supposedly dead conscience twisted hard within him. His stomach plummeted. "Again, I'm sorry. Well, you've got my number. Give me a call, and we can work something out."

"I'm afraid I don't have your number anymore. I must have used it to mop up the—" Jacqui broke off as someone else came over to them. "Mr. Forbes, thank you again for the opportunity."

"Not at all, Miss Dorne. Thank you for a very enjoyable presentation. We'll get back to your office by Monday at the latest. May I walk you to your car?"

"Yes. Thank you." Snapping the laptop case shut, Jacqui gathered her things. She inclined her head in Liam's direction. "Mr. Page."

"Miss Dorne." Liam watched as she followed Justin from the room. He headed back to the staff room to pick up his things and then out to the car. He dumped his papers on the roof and pulled the keys from his pocket.

"Mr. Page." Her voice rang like a bell in the evening haze.

Liam twisted around. "Miss Dorne. We'll have to stop meeting like this. People are going to talk."

Jacqui walked over to his car.

Liam watched the way her hips moved and wondered if she knew the effect she was having on him. Then he chided himself for such thoughts. He had principles, after all. "Nice wheels," Landscape architecture must pay better than teaching.

"Thank you. Uh, I'm afraid I used all the serviettes to try and save the laptop. So I no longer have your number."

"No problem. I can give it to you again." He

pulled his diary from his jacket pocket and tore out a sheet. He scribbled the number down and handed it to her.

"Thank you." She folded the paper and slipped it into her bag.

"You're welcome." He turned to go, and then turned back. "Can I buy you dinner by way of an apology?" The words were out before he even realized his mind had formed them. What was he thinking? Or not thinking as the case may be.

"Dinner?" She sounded as surprised by his invitation as he was.

He studied her, not sure if he wanted her to accept or not. "Dinner, it's usually the last meal of the day."

A wry smile crossed her lips. "I know that. I can't do tonight."

"What about tomorrow? Say seven o'clock? I could pick you up."

"What about your wife? Won't she object to you taking me out to dinner?"

Liam looked at her. He hadn't said anything about being married. "My wife?"

Jacqui nodded to his left hand. "You're married. I don't date married men."

"Oh…" Liam hoped Sally would understand. "This isn't a *date*, it's an apology."

"Are you sure?"

"Yes, I'm quite sure. Shall I pick you up?"

"How about I meet you at six? Is pizza all right?"

"Pizza sounds great. Do you know the restaurant on the Riverside?"

"I know it. I'll see you tomorrow, Mr. Page."

"Until then, Miss Dorne."

She walked back to her car and drove away.

Liam unlocked the car and shoved his papers onto the back seat. *What am I thinking? I don't need dates. Especially with a woman who could distract me from what I need to do ensure that what happened to Sally never happens again.* Another portion of his brain kicked in. *It's not a date, it's an apology. Right. And if she believes that, then I'm a monkey's uncle.*

****

Liam let himself into his empty flat and put his keys on the counter along with the papers. He'd mark them later. He automatically paused, waiting for the "Hi darling, I'm in the kitchen/living room/upstairs," which never came. Not that he had an upstairs anymore. He'd sold the house and bought something small, unable to live in a home filled with memories.

Where he lived now was technically a maisonette. A house divided into two halves, he owned the ground floor. An older couple he hardly ever saw owned the floor above him.

Shrugging out of his jacket he hung it up, only for it to slide to the floor. He grunted with annoyance, picked it up and shoved it hard onto the coat hook. He glared at it, daring it to fall off again. Was the rest of the day going to go downhill, too?

His steps echoed in the empty hall, emphasizing his loneliness. He'd been alone for what seemed like a lifetime, although it wasn't. Alone with his memories and his nightmares and thoughts of what used to be. Sally had been the only woman he loved, his sun, moon and stars, the one he wanted to live with forever. Until someone decided on a whim to take her away.

Why? The familiar question welled within him.

Not that he'd get an answer. There was no one to give him an answer. God had chosen to turn His back on him and Sally and the others and let them die. And that was unforgivable. They were out there doing God's work and that was how He repaid them. Shouting and screaming at God had made no difference. Neither had begging, or making promises, or trying to strike a bargain. So he had turned his back on the God who'd abandoned him.

His hands curled into a fist. And now, today, he'd met a woman who reminded him so much of Sally. An incredibly, insanely beautiful woman—full of innocence and youth and totally unaware of the allure she exuded. And he didn't just meet her once, when he stupidly ruined a very expensive piece of equipment, but three times. For some inexplicable reason, she kept wandering back into his path. And then he did something even more stupid and asked her out!

Asked out a total stranger, yet someone his body seemed to feel an instant attraction for. He dug his fingers into his palms and groaned. He didn't need his body betraying Sally's memory or betraying him, come to that. That part of his life was over.

And he definitely didn't need God, not that he believed in Him, dangling a possible future in front of him like a carrot. He detested carrots. He knew what he was missing without having it rubbed in his face— home, wife, family, love. That wasn't going to happen. He would never know love or family again. He was cursed, destined to be alone.

What he did need was a drink. The one thing guaranteed to numb the pain and torment flooding the hole where his soul used to reside. Walking to the lounge he undid the bottle on the sideboard and poured a glass. Raising it to his lips, he was about to down it, when his gaze fell on the photo on the mantelpiece.

Sally. She hated him drinking. She knew he had a drinking problem—OK was a recovering alcoholic before she married him. He struggled with what it said in the Bible about drinking. And with some Christians drinking and some spurning it, he was even more confused at times. When he first became a Christian, not drinking was easy, but the craving was still there and one drink with a friend led to another and another.

With Sally's help he'd gone to AA classes and climbed on the wagon. He'd be lying if he said it was easy. It was one of the hardest things he'd ever done, but Sally had been there every step of the way. Loving him, supporting him, not letting him give in. She refused to have anything remotely alcoholic in the house—not even the food flavorings. Shop-bought Christmas puddings were also banned, she made her own nonalcoholic version.

He started drinking again after she'd gone. Gone. Left him. Passed on. Passed over. Died. All euphemisms for what was such an ugly, heart breaking, soul destroying word. Just a small word with such massive repercussions that had frozen his soul and stopped his life.

Murdered.

He raised the glass in a mock salute and swallowed.

Sally was dead. Slaughtered in a terrorist attack on the mission field, in a massacre that hadn't even made the news here. And he'd barely escaped with his life. He'd tried to save the others, but had failed in the attempt. Phantom pain from the scars shot through him and he rubbed his chin.

Nothing he said or thought could change the fact she was gone. But there was something he could do. And when he caught up with the people responsible, they'd pay. Revenge was a dish best served cold and vengeance would be his. No matter how many years it took.

He ran his fingers over Sally's picture, a sudden surge of guilt filling him over this dinner "not-a-date" he'd arranged. He ought to explain to Sally.

"Her name's Miss Dorne. Jacqui Dorne. And it's not a date. It's just an apology dinner. Nothing more—I knocked a vase of flowers over her computer and killed it. You don't mind, do you? It's been eighteen months, but I still love you." He paused. "You know, I've never even looked twice at another woman before today. I don't know if it's just that she reminds me of you, or because I feel guilty for ruining her laptop, or what. But, yeah, I looked at her twice. More than twice."

Liam set the photo down and looked at the glass. It was empty already. He picked up the bottle and poured another. Then he stared at the photo. "Fine, you're right. No more." He put the glass down and sighed. "I should go mark those papers."

He turned, seeing in his mind the figure on the swing. He gave her one final push and ran around the other side to smile at her. Only this time the hair flying around her face was long and dark, not long and fair.

Another stab of guilt pierced him for letting this woman he didn't know get under his skin and into his thoughts. He had no right to think of anyone but Sally.

****

Jacqui washed the casserole dish and handed it to Holly. "So what's Kyle doing tonight? Not still cutting hair at this hour?"

Holly shook her head as she dried the dish. "No, he's preaching."

Surprise filled her. "Preaching? I didn't think he was into that side of the ministry."

Holly nodded. "Pastor Jack asked him to speak at the old folk's home on Crescent Road. He was looking forward to it."

Jacqui smiled. "Well good for him. Of course he might end up doing it forever now."

"I don't think he'll mind. It's only once a month." Holly paused. "So how did the presentation go? You were a bundle of nerves when we spoke on the phone last night."

She looked at the bubbles coating her hands as she cleaned the saucepan. "And with good reason, my whole career is resting on this one." She scrubbed hard at the pan before setting it on the draining board. "It was fine, eventually. There was this one guy, Liam Page. We met in the cafe at lunchtime when he knocked a vase of flowers over onto my laptop and killed it. He teaches at the school and spent the entire presentation making eyes at me before asking me out at the end of it."

"Oh, aye? What's he like, then?"

"He's tall, dark, and handsome, has a cute beard and looks like a movie star."

"Very nice. You know that's a pretty romantic way to meet someone. He throws flowers all over you."

"You're a fine one to talk. You thought Kyle was a mass murderer when you first met him." Jacqui flicked soap bubbles at Holly.

"Hey, in my defense, it was a dark night and he accosted me while I was lying under the car trying to fix it." She winked. "But you know it is kind of funny meeting someone like that."

"Please don't look at me like that. I already got the "say it with flowers" joke from Eve, more than once, and it wasn't funny then. Besides, there is one very big hitch in any matchmaking plans you might have. He's married."

"Oh." Holly looked at her, aghast. "Married?"

Jacqui nodded. It sounded worse when she spoke it aloud. She needed to distract Holly. "Yes, he's married. The good ones always are. We can't all land the perfect man, you know. And they don't all save us from serial killers, either."

The smile on Holly's face lit her eyes. "Yeah, Kyle was rather heroic, wasn't he?"

"Is Kyle's head as big as it ought to be?" Jacqui teased her friend.

Holly laughed. "He gets rid of spiders, too. Want me to send him over?"

Jacqui handed her another dish. "It's fine. I'm not scared of spiders."

"So this Liam…what does he teach?"

"He's head of English at the secondary school. And please no jokes about it being ironic that a Mr. Page teaches English. Eve's done that one to death, as well. He offered to pay for the laptop, so I guess he can't be all bad. And he's taking me to dinner tomorrow to apologize."

Consternation flooded Holly's face. "But you said he's married. Jac, is that the wisest option? You don't want to give him the wrong idea."

"I'm not. I made it perfectly clear it's just dinner and nothing more. He looked flustered when I asked if his wife would mind. He was adamant she wouldn't."

"Hmmm, must be a very understanding woman then. Not sure I'd like Kyle taking another woman to dinner. Not even to apologize. Unless he took me along, too, then I guess it'd be all right. Where are you going?"

"He's taking me to the pizza place on the Riverside. Why? What are you thinking?"

"Maybe I could get Kyle to take me there. That way if this Liam makes a move you don't like, Kyle can do his superhero bit and save you, too."

Jacqui chuckled at the image of Kyle in tights, shorts and a cape that sprang into her mind. "That's not necessary, but if you two just happened to be there around six or so, it'd be good. I'm meeting him there— figured if I took my own car I could leave whenever I wanted and he wouldn't have to drive me home."

"All right, we'll be there. Just promise me you won't do anything you'll regret."

"I promise. Liam is a nice enough guy, but he's married. I'm not going to cross that line, no matter what."

3

Liam glanced up from the menu to the woman sitting opposite him. He smiled, still surprised she agreed to come and still unable to believe he'd actually asked her. *Keep in mind this is just an apology and nothing else.* "What would you like?"

Jacqui smiled back. "I think I'll have the Hawaiian."

Does she know how pretty she is when she smiles? I don't suppose she does. "That happens to be my favorite. Shall I order a large and we can share?"

"Sounds good. Can we have onion rings as well?"

"Of course, with potato wedges?"

Her smile grew. "Is there any other way to eat pizza?"

"If you're my brother-in-law, yes there is. Jared eats it with a knife and fork."

Jacqui's laugh was beautiful like the rest of her. What was it about this woman that made him feel so out of control? And why? He didn't want to get involved with anyone, especially someone who reminded him so much of the past.

The waitress came over and he ordered the pizza, a side of onion rings, potato wedges, and salad. He glanced at Jacqui. "What would you like to drink?"

"Diet lemonade."

Shaking his head in amusement, he turned back to the waitress. "A diet lemonade and a regular one, both with ice and a slice of lemon, please." He grinned at Jacqui after ordering.

"What?"

"We're having pizza, which is about as fattening as you can get, never mind the onion rings and potato wedges, and you want *diet* lemonade?"

"I just got a taste for the diet stuff when I worked abroad."

"I don't like the aftertaste. Give me the sugar and calories any time." Liam watched as she beamed and waved at a couple sitting three tables away from them. "Friends of yours?"

Jacqui nodded. "That's Holly and Kyle. They go to the same church I do. They're getting married in the autumn."

"Cool."

She smiled. "They're fortunate. Being married beats being alone like I am."

Liam shifted slightly in his seat. He really didn't want to discuss marriage and its pros or cons tonight. He was as alone as she seemed to be. He changed the subject. "You said you worked abroad. What did you do?"

"I spent six months in Africa, doing design work for a mission in a remote area..."

Africa? His breath caught fading her voice into the background. *Did she know I was there?*

Then reason took over. Africa was a huge continent, made up of at least fifty countries—more if you include the ones that are technically part of Europe, even though they are on the African plate. She probably wasn't even in the same country as him.

Her voice resurfaced. "...and then the company funding the project ran out of money, and we had to come home before we finished."

He picked up his coaster turning it over on its side and twisting it end over end on the table. "Know how that is. The credit crunch is affecting everything. Which mission?"

"One of the small ones in Botswana. A group of us were sent out by my church." Her fingers went to her necklace.

That was the second time she'd mentioned church in as many minutes. His gaze followed the movement of her hands as she toyed with the necklace. "It's pretty."

"Thanks. My parents gave it to me for my birthday."

The drinks came, and he set his coaster back down on the table. He smiled at the waitress. "Thank you." He picked up his glass and sipped the soda, turning his attention back to Jacqui. "So tell me about yourself."

Her fingers drew lines in the condensation on her glass. "There's not much to tell. I'm a landscape architect. I have a bungalow, a cat, and a car."

"No brothers or sisters?"

"Nope, just me."

"What about your parents? Are they local?"

She paused for several seconds. Were her parents a touchy subject? She took a deep breath, her fingers crushing the glass in her right hand. "They died in the Whitgate train crash last year."

Liam reached across the table and took her left hand, wishing he hadn't asked. "I'm sorry."

"I blamed myself for a while."

He frowned. "I'm sorry? How can the train crash be your fault? I thought it was caused by the driver taking the bend too fast." No sooner than the words fell from his lips, than he immediately brought himself up sharply. *That's rather hypocritical isn't it? You blame yourself for Sally's death even though you didn't pull the trigger.*

Jacqui didn't meet his gaze, her eyes sparkling with tears. "They were coming home from holiday. Normally we'd have all gone, but I had to work and needed the car. That's why they were on the train. I was waiting on the platform for them, and I saw the whole accident."

"I'm sorry. I shouldn't have asked." The spear in his soul dug deeper seeing her tears threatening to fall. He'd made her cry.

Her teeth worried her bottom lip as she spoke, her gaze fixed on the glass. "The train came around the bend at full speed. It started to tilt and kept going. It derailed, and the carriages crashed into each other, piling up like a heap of matchsticks. Their carriage ended on the platform. It stopped only yards from where I was standing."

He squeezed her hand, and then rubbed his thumb over the back of it. He hoped the simple touch would offer some modicum of comfort. He knew what it was like to lose someone close to you. Someone that you loved more than life itself. And just as people didn't know what to say around him, he, too, found himself lost for words.

"I thought I was going to die. You know those dreams when you're rooted to the spot and can't move. It was like that. I just stood there, watching the train come hurtling towards me, every muscle in my body frozen."

He waited for her to meet his gaze before speaking. "I'm really sorry for your loss. The TV coverage was horrendous, but to have been there and known those involved must have been far worse."

She bit her lip and closed her eyes for a moment. "It was rough for a while, but they say time heals, and I have my memories of them."

"Sometimes that's all we have left."

"You sound like you're speaking from personal experience."

I don't need this. Why is fate throwing us together like this? It's a simple apology over dinner. I don't want or need another woman in my life. The coincidences—for that was the only word for them—were piling up. She had worked on the same continent and had lost her family. Only difference was he still had his twin sister, his parents and his elder brother.

"Mr. Page?" Her soft voice brought him back to the conversation.

"Yes. I uh... I lost someone I cared about."

"Was it someone close?" She broke off. "I'm sorry. I shouldn't ask."

He took a long drink and set the glass down, shaking his head. "It's all right. Just something I'm having trouble coming to terms with."

"It must have been something pretty bad."

Perhaps she'd understand. After all she'd been there. His brother and his twin sister, whilst they did what they could, they didn't really know, couldn't possibly know what it was like. The soul wrenching loss that encompassed every part of you, swallowed you, up and never spat you out. Miss Dorne's tears showed him that she knew; that she was acquainted with the darkness of grief.

"Yeah, it was. It was my—"

"Here you go," The waitress came over with the

pizza and Liam broke off, the moment gone. He let her serve them and waited until she left before smiling at Jacqui. "Bon appétit."

"Thank you. So, you know about me and I know almost nothing about you. That doesn't seem very fair. Do you have any brothers or sisters?"

He picked up a slice. "Yes, I have one of each. My sister, actually she's my twin sister, Niamh. Not that we share the same birthday. I was born ten minutes before midnight, and she was born ten minutes after. We tend to celebrate on the same day though. Most years we use mine and every fourth year we use hers. She's adamant her age only increases every four years as she was born on February twenty-ninth. She's a barrel of laughs when she's not working. Then she's just scary in that black outfit and white wig of hers."

"Sounds intriguing."

"She's a hot-shot barrister for the Crown Prosecution Service. Senior prosecutor or something like that. To hear her tell it, criminals tremble when they hear she's prosecuting them and either admit their guilt or run for the hills. My brother Patrick works in security. Mum and Dad live the other side of town. I have a small one bedroom ground floor maisonette, no cats, and no dogs. I like riding, hate football, and love teaching." He avoided mentioning Sally.

"Hate football? Do you prefer rugby?"

"I enjoy watching rugby. I can't play it any longer, knee injury. But I prefer tennis anyway. I'm pretty good at it, or I used to be. Haven't played in a while. Niamh and Patrick have never beaten me, although they both spent years trying."

"And you're modest with it." Jacqui teased him. "I always wanted a brother or sister. Must have been fun growing up. Are you the eldest, youngest?"

"I rank second. Patrick's the eldest, then me, then Niamh." He paused. "We hale from Belfast originally. We moved here when I was ten. We all kept our accents."

"So being Irish, I'd guess you'd be Catholic?"

He shook his head and studied the pizza in his hand. What was it with her and religion?

"Irish, yes. Catholic no. We lived in the protestant side of Belfast, but I'm not anything. God and I aren't on speaking terms anymore, and I can't see that changing."

"What happened, Liam?"

He could feel her gaze on him without looking up. It was as if she could see inside him. Her x-ray vision tearing at his soul, unburying and breaking open the casket of grief and black memories.

Why had he asked about her family and what happened? It was only natural she'd want to know about his and Sally is…was such an integral part of that. Liam stared at the pizza, not wanting this conversation, but at the same time knowing he had to answer her question. His gaze shifted to his wedding ring. He gave a long sigh.

"Sally." His tone was blunt. He needed to keep in control here. He twisted the ring digging it into the skin at the base of his finger, the pain jolting the memories from his mind.

"Sally? Is she your wife?"

"Was. She was my wife."

Her brow furrowed. And she tilted her head as if prompting him for more. How did she do that? He'd successfully not spoken of Sally for over a year. Not even Niamh had managed to get him to express his grief and here in the space of less than an hour Jacqui had him wanting to pour out his soul.

She gave a reassuring smile. Jacqui had lost her parents, she too was grieving. She would understand. At least he hoped she would. And if she didn't, well it wasn't like he was going to see her again.

"She looked a little like you, only her hair was blonde. Maybe it was just the fact she also wore a cross around her neck, too. I'm sorry. I'm meant to be apologizing for ruining your laptop and all your work. Instead here I am telling you—"

Jacqui's hand covered his. "It's fine. Go on."

He took a deep breath. "It's ironic. Niamh wanted me to go see a shrink and talk. Needless to say I refused. Yet, you...I hardly know you and something..." his voice trailed off.

"Sometimes it's easier to talk to someone who knows what it's like." Her soft tone encouraged him. "Someone who's walking the same path you are."

Liam held her gaze and inclined his head a fraction. Was he as easy to read as a book? "Sally and I had been married for three years. Eighteen months ago, we went to Endarra to work in the mission there. She'd always wanted to be a missionary, so we saved every penny we had and got accepted by a mission society for short term work. If we liked it, we decided we'd do it full time. It would be an adventure, a way to serve God and teach English to kids who wouldn't otherwise learn it." He bit his lip.

Jacqui squeezed his hand. "If it's too hard you don't have to tell me."

"No, I...I haven't even told Niamh all the details. Actually...you'll be the first."

"Then I'm honored." A slight smile turned up the

corners of her mouth. "It seems to be a day for firsts. I've never spoken about my parents' deaths either."

He swallowed hard. That made them even. And it helped a little. "It was the end of our second week. Sally loved it there. She loved the scenery, the people, the kids, everything about the place. She'd wake each morning with a smile on her face, a song in her heart and a prayer on her lips. She loved telling the kids about God and how Jesus died to save them. She was in her element. It was mid-morning — a Friday. All the kids sat at her feet listening to her. She'd just finished teaching them the song about the wise man who built his house upon a rock with the actions and was telling them the Bible story to go with it."

Liam paused, feeling his muscles tense as if anticipating the wounds. "Gunmen burst into the compound. We had a couple of guns for protection, but we couldn't get to them. Sally stood in front of the kids and tried to reason with the men, but they...they killed her. They fired at random," his voice roughened. "I...I was shot three times. I tried to reach her..."

Jacqui didn't say a word. Her face wore an expression of horror and the same grief he saw every morning in his mirror. She knew about witnessing the death of those one loved.

"Sally died in my arms," he struggled to keep the raw emotion out of his voice. "The British Embassy shipped the survivors home once the local hospital had patched us up enough to fly. I should have taken better care of her, and God should have protected His missionaries."

"I'm so sorry."

"I haven't spoken to God since. Don't see the point. He doesn't care for me, so why should I care for

Him?" Liam felt pressure and clenched his jaw tight. Now she knew. He was a failure.

Taking a deep breath, he pushed his chair back. "I'll be right back." Getting up, he headed for the men's room. He just need a moment to breathe, to recompose himself, to tamp down the anger and self-loathing that threatened to spill over every time he thought about Sally and how he failed her.

****

Jacqui watched him go and buried her face in her hands. His story was heartbreaking, his pain so palpable it threatened to overwhelm her. She'd lost her parents—her bedrock and entire family yes, but he'd lost his soul mate and his faith. He was truly alone.

Jacqui felt the lump in her throat, and touched the cross there, knowing she still had God.

"Jacqui?" Holly's gentle voice made her look up. A pair of concerned filled eyes stared at her and a tissue pressed into her hand. "What's wrong? What happened? Did he make you cry?"

Jacqui looked beyond Holly to where Kyle sat on the edge of his chair, his serviette in hand, ready to get up if needed. She turned her gaze back to Holly, swallowing hard, and rubbing the tissue over her eyes.

"Kyle will follow him to the gents and warn him off if you want, while I go home with you. Then Kyle'll come pick me up later."

She hugged Holly tightly. What would she do without friends like them? "I'm fine…he…I just need a minute."

"You're not fine. 'Fine' doesn't sit in the middle of a pizza joint sobbing into a Hawaiian, wedges, and onion rings. Did he hurt you? Did he say something to upset you?"

A waft of aftershave filled her senses.

"Jacqui?" Kyle's deep voice jerked her head upright. "Do I need to go punch his lights out?"

A wry smile flitted on her lips for an instant. "That's not very Christian of you."

"Made you smile though."

Jacqui nodded. "Thanks for the offer, but no you don't." She grabbed control and hung on. "Things just got a little intense that's all. We were talking about family, and I was telling him about Mum and Dad and the train crash. Stuff I've never told anyone before. Don't ask me why I could open up to a complete stranger and not you guys, but...I was there," she finished in a whisper.

Holly gripped her hand tightly. "Jac?"

"On the platform when the train crashed. It came to a halt yards from my feet."

They enveloped her in a hug.

"Talk about coming out in public. Anyway. I told him about that and he told me about his wife." She noticed her friends give each other a long 'I told you so' look and shook her head. "She's dead. She was murdered on the mission field last year some time."

Holly's face fell and even Kyle looked sick. Too close to home for the both of them. Holly had almost been the first and last victim of the Headley Cross serial killer last Christmas and Kyle's previous girlfriend had been the second victim.

Jacqui gripped both their hands tightly. "I'm sorry, I didn't think."

Kyle recovered first. "It's fine. We can't walk on eggshells forever." His intent gaze burned into her.

"Are you sure you're all right?"

"I'm fine. Don't let your pizza get cold. And Liam will be back soon."

"OK. But the first sign of any trouble and I'll be over here."

"Thank you. But I'll be fine." She smiled and watched them go back to their table. She tucked the tissue into her sleeve and hoped that too many people weren't watching her very public meltdown.

Liam had been gone a while. She hoped he was all right.

****

Liam splashed cold water on his face. *Get a grip. She doesn't need to see this. At least I can honestly tell Niamh I've talked to someone next time she brings it up.* He took a couple of deep breaths, then dried his hands and face and headed back into the restaurant.

He expected her to be gone, but she was sitting there.

He slid into his seat. "Guess that's kind of ruined the evening. I'm sorry."

Jacqui shook her head. "No, it hasn't. I'm still hungry...unless you don't want dinner anymore."

"Dinner's fine. I'm still hungry." Liam glanced across the room and noticed Kyle watching him. "Your friend is keeping an eye on me. He must think I upset you."

Jacqui followed his gaze. "Holly did come over and check when she saw me crying, but I assured her I was fine."

"I didn't mean to make you upset, Miss Dorne. I'm sorry."

"It's Jacqui. Miss Dorne makes me sound old." She held a hand across to him.

Liam smiled and took it. "Liam. It's a pleasure to meet you. Are you sure I've not ruined your appetite?"

"I'm sure. Actually, I owe you my thanks. For getting me to open up and talk."

"As I do you."

"Besides, there are still heaps of things we can talk about." She picked up her pizza.

He picked up his own and bit into it. "Like what?" he asked around a mouthful.

"Did your mother never tell you not to talk with your mouth full?"

A faint smile crossed his face. "All the time, but I didn't listen to her about that stuff. None of us did."

"Nor did I. Well, I haven't told you what I call my cat."

Liam swallowed and picked up his glass. "Schrödinger?"

"That's a good one. I didn't think of that. Nope, he's called Mandu."

"Mandu?" The penny dropped, and he chuckled. "Cat-mandu. Oh, that's very clever."

"He was Atastrophe for a while, but I preferred Mandu in the end."

He groaned. "That's even worse. Mind you, I used to have fish when I was a kid. We called them Bit and Bot, and all the little ones were Tiddlywinks."

"I thought I was bad calling my dolls after the characters on a TV show I watched when I was five."

"I called my teddy Big Ted." He finished his slice of pizza and reached for another the same time she did. His fingers touched hers, and a spark of electricity flowed through his hand and straight to his heart.

Their gazes met. He smiled awkwardly, not wanting the physical reaction coursing through his body. He couldn't explain it. The last woman to affect him like this was Sally. He didn't want anyone else. This was a mistake.

It must be down to the emotional bond they just shared of talking about their respective losses. Nothing more. That he could live with.

Perhaps.

Jacqui looked at him. Had she felt it too? Her smile reached her eyes. "Guess we're both softies, then."

He nodded, offering Jacqui another piece of pizza. "So what do you plan to do with your life? Are you happy being a landscape architect?"

"Yes, I am."

"What can you see yourself doing in ten years' time?"

"I don't know. Become CEO one day maybe, or go back to Africa and finish that orphanage. What about you? Would you ever go back and teach out there again?"

He shook his head. "No plans to go back out there at all. I'm settled here. Is it possible to get higher than head of department? Other than running my own school, that is." He felt guilty for the lie about not planning to return to Africa, but his plans had to remain secret.

Jacqui winked at him. "I'll design the grounds, and you can run it. We'd make a good team."

Liam laughed and raised his glass. "I'll drink to that." As she chinked her glass against his, the light shone in her eyes, and her beauty struck him with the force of a sledge hammer. What would it be like to kiss her? He shook his head, mentally slapping himself.

Enough, time to get out of here before his resolve shattered. He finished his pizza.

"Thank you for a lovely evening, but I should go. I have a lot of paperwork to do before tomorrow." She pushed her plate aside.

He nodded. "You will let me know about the laptop?"

Jacqui nodded as she stood. "I will. Goodnight."

"Goodnight." Liam watched her leave and sat for a moment. He didn't like the way he felt.

The woman had moved him. He barely knew her, and he'd told her things he hadn't told anyone—not even his twin. Sliding his hand into his jacket, he pulled out his wallet and went to pay the bill. Perhaps marking homework would get his mind off Jacqui.

4

Jacqui looked up as Eve came over to her desk. "Good morning."

Eve sat on the corner of the desk and looked at her critically. "You look a little pale. Are you sick?"

"No, just tired. I didn't sleep much last night."

"Heavy date?"

Jacqui dismissed that idea with a wave of her hand. "Nothing like that at all—just dinner with a friend. Holly and Kyle were at the next table. Have I.T. got back to you about the laptop yet?"

"Yes. Good news is they can fix it. Bad news is it'll be cheaper to simply replace it."

Jacqui groaned and buried her head in her hands. "Great. Better give Liam the bad news, I guess."

Her friend nudged her. "Liam is it now? Remember that married man conversation."

Jacqui fixed her eyes on Eve. "You and Holly both gave me the same lecture. He's widowed, he told me last night."

"Last night? No wonder you're tired."

"I was home by nine-thirty and in bed by ten." She didn't have to state the *alone*.

Eve knew very well where she stood on that score.

"It was just dinner, nothing more." She took the paper Eve offered. "I'll ring him and give him the bad news." As Eve crossed the room, Jacqui sighed and pulled the folded piece of paper from her bag. She ran her fingers over it before picking up the phone and dialing.

The phone rang several times. "Hi, this is Liam. I can't get to the phone right now, please leave a message and I'll get back to you."

She couldn't leave a message like this on his voice mail. It'd be better if she spoke to him in person. "Hi, Liam, it's Jacqui Dorne from the Jekyll Foundation." She left her number. "If you could ring me back when you get a chance it'd be good. Thank you."

Lunch came and went. Arriving back from a meeting, she found a note on her desk. She'd missed Liam's call by ten minutes. Oh well, she'd try again in a bit. He should be out of class by then. She looked down at the design on her desk and picked up the pencil. That top corner wasn't quite right.

"Jacqui, you have a visitor." Lost in her work, the voice made her start.

Jacqui looked past Eve to the figure standing in her office doorway. What was he doing here? "Liam...aren't you meant to be teaching?"

"It's almost five PM. I thought I'd call in on my way home on the off chance you were still in the office. I take it this is about the laptop."

Jacqui hadn't realized it was so late. Where had the afternoon gone? She gestured to the chair the other side of her desk. "Have a seat."

Liam raised an eyebrow as he sat down. "That bad, huh?"

She nodded. "It'll cost more to fix than buy a new one. I'm sorry."

"Don't be sorry, it's my fault, not yours." He reached into his jacket pocket and pulled out his check book. "If you just let me know how much a new one costs and who to make it out to, I'll pay you now."

She slid the paper over the desk and noticed his expression change as he read it. "If it's too much then—"

"I said I'd pay for the damage." He wrote the check and tore it from the book. "Here you go."

"Thank you." Jacqui took it, feeling heat flood her fingers as his hand touched hers. She hadn't imagined it last night, but it wasn't going to happen. He was mourning his wife. Plus which he was angry at God and by his own admission wasn't a Christian. Or at least not any more.

Liam held her gaze. "What are you thinking?"

She raised an eyebrow, his touch sending goose bumps running down her arm and straight to the pit of her stomach. "What makes you think that I'm thinking anything?"

"Either you're thinking, or I'm more off base than I've been in a long time."

"I was just thinking how much I enjoyed last night, Liam. Far more than I should have done."

Confusion crossed his face. "Why? Aren't you allowed to enjoy dinner with a friend? Does your church have rules against that?"

"No, no, nothing like that. It's just you're married—widowed—and obviously still very much in love with your wife and I can't be, I don't want to be the other—"

Liam cut her off. "You're not the other woman. Yes, I do still love Sally. Part of me always will. And like I said, she wouldn't mind me taking a friend to dinner."

Jacqui warmed under his gaze. That was the second time he'd said that now. "Is that what we are then? Friends?"

"I'd like to be."

She could hear the sincerity in his voice.

"I mean, you have every right not to want to be, but—"

"No." It was her turn to cut him off. "I'd like that."

"Me, too."

The phone rang.

"Jacqui Dorne...Hello, Mr. Forbes." She listened as he spoke. Joy bubbled up inside her, spilling into a grin. "Thank you very much. That sounds great. Sure, I'll see you on Monday." She hung up and looked at Liam. "I got the contract. I start Monday."

"That's wonderful. Congratulations."

"Thank you."

"What are you doing tonight?"

"Nothing." Actually she did nothing most nights, but wasn't about to admit it.

"I see. In that case, can I tempt you to join me for dinner? There's an Indian place on the High Street I've been meaning to try for ages. We could go celebrate. Unless you'd prefer Chinese?"

Jacqui hesitated for a moment, and then nodded. "Thank you. I'd like that. And I adore Indian food. Can't beat a nice chicken madras and naan bread with pilau rice."

****

Candlelight glittered off the glasses. Liam picked his up and smiled at Jacqui.

Her hair was piled atop her head and fixed with a pearl clasp, with soft strands falling from the sides, framing her face. He was no expert, but her perfume smelled French and expensive.

He raised his glass. "To your new tender. May your work be as good as the plans look."

Jacqui chinked her glass against his. "I'll do my best."

Liam took a large drink of his wine. Even though it was the house special, it wasn't bad. He looked at the apple juice Jacqui had chosen and wondered if she ever drank. Sally hadn't. Guilt twisted within him. The wine in his mouth tasted sour and he grimaced as he swallowed it. With Sally it was easy. Maybe…maybe it had all been her and not him. She was a wonderful, wholesome Christian woman and he was a drunken slob. He deserved to die out there. She didn't.

"Are you all right?"

He nodded. "I'm fine. Sally didn't like me drinking. I stopped while we were married."

"Why start again?"

"I don't know. To forget, I guess."

Jacqui held his gaze, no matter how hard he tried to look elsewhere. "Wouldn't it be a more fitting tribute to her to stay sober? She shouldn't be forgotten."

"It's not Sally I want to forget." His tone was sharper than he intended. "It's her dying in my arms."

Jacqui put her fork down and looked at her plate. "You're not the only one who lost someone," she told him. "But we don't all dive into a bottle."

"I'm sorry. I didn't mean to upset you. Forgive me?"

She looked up and nodded slowly. "God saved you for a reason, Liam. And it wasn't to drink to forget."

"You're right. I'll stop. It's what she wanted." He

put the glass down. He started eating again. He wasn't going to add the only reason he survived was so he could kill the people responsible, she didn't need to know that. "What time Monday do you start?"

"First thing. I get to meet the caretaker and check out the grounds. I take measurements, that kind of thing. Then it's back to the office to work on finalizing the plans and drawings for a day or two and then go back to Mr. Forbes. After that, the fun part begins—the actual planting, landscaping and so on."

"Sounds like a lot of work. Don't you delegate the planting and stuff to other people? I can't imagine you getting your hands dirty."

A smile lit her face. "I do have a team of people that help, but I love planting. That's why I got into this. There's something about being close to nature. It's peaceful. You should try it."

Liam shook his head. "Marking homework and mud isn't a good combination."

Jacqui laughed. "You'd have to give yourself detention and that wouldn't be any good."

His laughter joined hers. "No, but the kids would love it."

She nodded as she put down her knife and fork. "They would. That was lovely, thank you."

"You're welcome. Would you like dessert?"

"Desserts are overrated."

"Desserts are also 'stressed' backwards."

"So they are." She patted her stomach. "But I'm full. Anything else would spoil it."

"Then how about a walk along the river to the bridge?"

"That sounds wonderful."

****

They strolled along the river and Jacqui wondered if he'd take her hand. She wasn't sure if she was relieved or disappointed when he didn't. Moonlight reflected off the water and as they reached the bridge, Liam began searching on the ground by the bushes. "What are you doing?"

"Looking for pooh sticks."

"I'm sorry?" She looked at him as if he'd grown a second head. "Is that like looking for those little green pixie things that guard pots of gold?"

"I said pooh sticks, not leprechauns. Though I can look for those as well if you like, Miss Jacqui, only they only tend to come out when there's a rainbow."

His Irish accent made her giggle and sent ripples of joy running through her. She'd never found regional accents particularly attractive, but his was such an integral part of him, that she barely noticed it now. Except when he used a turn of phrase or a word that was more Irish than others. She had a sudden vision of him on hand and knees, searching under the hedges for little green men, and it was tempting to ask him to do so just for the fun of it.

He tilted his head in a particularly charming way and winked. "You do know what pooh sticks are?"

Pooh sticks were a simple game involving a race between two sticks both dropped in to a river at the same time. "I do. But it's a kids' game."

"Then here you go." He handed her a stick. "I love pooh sticks. I will not have it mocked," he added sternly. "Or I may have to give you a detention."

Jacqui winked and fired off an imitation salute. "Then I will not mock it, sir. You'll need to remind me how to play. I haven't done it for years."

Liam moved to the side of the bridge, his footsteps clattering on the wooden slats. "We both drop the sticks at the same time. First one under the bridge and out the other side wins."

"You played it a lot by the sounds of it."

"Niamh loves playing this. Though she cheats somewhat."

"How on earth do you cheat at pooh sticks?"

"She chucks her stick in at an angle. I don't stand a chance of beating her."

"Well, I promise not to cheat." Jacqui smiled and leaned over the side. "On three. One, two, three."

She dropped the stick at the same time as Liam and then ran to the other side of the bridge. They both leaned over waiting. She caught her breath and then cheered as her stick came through first.

"Beginners luck." Liam said, and then laughed. "I'll win next time."

She looked at him. "Next time?"

He caught her gaze. "I'd like to see you again. It's what friends do, isn't it?"

Other than Eve, Holly and Kyle she didn't have any friends. And Holly and Kyle were more wrapped up in each other these days. Which was fair enough. The thought of having another friend was appealing. Even if he did drink and he didn't share her faith, but there would be no harm in being his friend. Perhaps God was trying to tell her she could help him somehow. "Yes. I'd like that too. Fine, you can win the next time…maybe."

"Or not as the case may be." Liam smiled. "What are you doing this weekend?"

"Tomorrow is the anniversary of the train crash.

There's a memorial service and unveiling of the plaque with the thirty-seven victims' names on it, which I'm going to attend. And then Sunday is church. There's a lunch this week as well." She paused briefly. "I don't suppose you'd like to come with me?"

"No. I can't, but thanks for the invitation. I've got tickets to the rugby on Sunday. It's a twelve-thirty kick off."

"Who's playing?"

"The Headley Tigers are playing Northampton Rovers in the challenge cup semi-final."

"Big game, then."

"Oh yeah. The winner goes through to Twickenham next month. Tickets for that will be like gold dust and probably cost just as much, but it'll be on the telly." He smiled. "So, shall I walk you to your car?"

"I'd like that. Thank you." She couldn't form any kind of attachment to this man.

He's not a Christian. He's off limits, like Vince. You know how that ended. Oh, Lord, I know what You said, and You were right. Draw me closer to You, and fill me with Your Spirit that I may live for You. Let me help Liam. His grief is still consuming him and there's something else, something dark. I wouldn't say evil, but there is darkness at work with in him. Work in him, Lord. Bring him back to You and use him for Your glory.

5

The phone rang.

Jacqui glanced up from where she lay curled on the bed and sighed as she pulled another tissue from the box, tempted not to answer it. It kept ringing. She reached out and grabbed it. "Holly, it's very kind of you, but I won't change my mind, no matter how many times you ring."

There was a pause before the very male, Irish lilt resounded in her ear.

"Then it's a very good job I'm not Holly, isn't it?"

Jacqui felt heat rise in her cheeks. "Oh, Liam, I'm sorry. Holly's rung five times trying to get me to go over there tonight."

"Ah. Well, I'm not after wanting you to go to Holly's. I actually rang to see how you were doing after the memorial service today."

Fresh tears stung her eyes and she closed them tightly. That was sweet of him. "It was…" Her voice wobbled and she struggled to keep the emotion from flooding out again. "It was really hard. So many ruined lives and people gone. But some good stuff. One couple met in the wreckage, and they're getting married next week."

"Hey, that's neat." His smile and concern came through. "Would you like some company?"

"Like I told Holly, I don't want—"

"And like I told you, I'm not Holly."

She blotted her eyes with the soggy tissue, sniffling again. "I know that. You look nothing like her. She doesn't have a beard for one thing."

"I don't even want you to talk if I come over. We'll walk around the lake. Watch the sun set behind the trees and just sit in silence. I just don't think that you should sit in that bungalow of yours moping." His voice deepened, indicating how concerned he was. So was Holly, but coming from Liam, someone she hardly knew, despite the couple of dinners they'd shared, it meant more.

"I'm not moping." The protest sounded weak even to her.

"So, you're not moping, you're sad, languishing, dejected."

"I am not—"

"Don't argue with me, Jacqui. You are, and it's not going to make you feel any better." His tone changed from concerned to firm.

Jacqui paused. He'd only known her three days, and yet he was spot on. "All right, yes, maybe I'm moping, a little."

"Let me pick you up. Where do you live?"

"You promise you're not an axe murderer?"

"I promise I'm not an axe murderer. And before you ask how I got your number, it was on the card I lifted from your desk yesterday."

Jacqui shook her head. "You're incorrigible." She took a deep breath. "Fifteen Raggleswood Crescent."

"I know it. I'll be there in ten."

****

True to his word, Liam pulled up in exactly ten minutes. As Jacqui opened the door, he had to restrain himself from not pulling her into the hug she so desperately needed. He settled for a smile and a sweeping bow. "Your carriage awaits, my lady."

Jacqui picked up her jacket and bag and followed him to the car. She looked at him, suspicion in her eyes. "You're not going to insist I talk?"

He shook his head. "No, not at all. We're going to sit in a companionable silence and watch the sun set."

Liam drove to the park, studiously ignoring the tears she shed on the way. He knew how painful anniversaries were, whether they were birthdays, wedding or death days. He also knew from experience that all Jacqui needed was someone to be there. He could do that, just like Niamh did for him. He parked next to the lake and got out. Going around the car, he opened the door.

"A poet once said that sunsets are magical and simply watching one can make someone feel better."

Jacqui got out, rubbing her eyes. "Right." Her voice still carried the echo of her tears.

"Don't believe it myself, any more than I believe in the luck o'the Irish, but that's what the poem said. Anyway, I have this bench right over here." Liam walked with her towards it. "I had it put here after Sally died. It's part of their 'adopt a bench' scheme. I just come and sit here sometimes. I wrote a poem to go on the plaque. Wanted something more personal than just her name and dates, you know."

Jacqui stood and read the plaque, her eyes glistening.

My love
And I would come
And sit here, feed the ducks
Or walk around the lake. Come spring,
Autumn, summer or winter, we'd be here.
Until the day Sally was taken
Away, leaving me just
Memories of
My love.

"That's lovely. Did you really write that?"

Liam nodded. "Yeah, it's the only poem I've ever written. She loved it here." He sat down and patted the space beside him. "Sit." He nodded as she sat and lapsed into silence. He gazed out over the water. Aware she was crying, Liam pulled out a tissue and offered it to her.

"Thanks." She buried her face in it.

He smiled. "It amazes me how women are always grateful for these, but never bother to ask if it's a clean one." He winked as she stiffened and pulled it away from her eyes looking at it.

"It's clean. My mother always told me to wear clean underwear and carry a clean hanky every time I go out. Though I use tissues so I don't have to launder and iron them."

Jacqui nodded, tears falling and shoulders shaking. Liam looked at her. For a moment he hesitated, remembering the vibrant, almost electric feeling that passed between them at each accidental touch. To instigate it and encourage that feeling would be wrong. But at the same time he couldn't just sit here and do nothing to comfort her. Offering her a hug was the right thing to do, and he had to put his feelings aside.

Taking a deep breath, he held out an arm. "Come here."

As she moved into his embrace and buried her face in his shoulder, he held her tightly, amazed at the force of emotion flooding her.

He'd mourned his wife, but never allowed himself to cry. Except the other night, at the pizza place when he'd shared his pain with this woman.

He was proud of the fact he hadn't cried, properly cried, since he was seven. Anger, on the other hand, he knew too well. He sat in silence, just holding her, looking out at the water and pondering why he'd almost let loose that night.

Eventually her sobs slowed and she looked up, her face red and swollen. "I'm sorry. I made your shirt all wet."

"Never apologize for showing your feelings. I'll dry. Besides, if you can't cry on a friend's shoulder who can you cry on?" He smiled at her as she sat up. "I'm happy to lend a shoulder whenever you need one."

"Thank you." She took the new tissue he offered.

He pulled his arm back, not wanting to impose the contact any longer than was comfortable. He smiled and pointed across the lake. "Watch—this is the best bit."

Jacqui followed his finger and gasped as a rush of gold swept across the lake as the setting sun hit the surface of the water. "Wow."

"That about sums it up."

The orange lit her eyes and something moved within him. This woman touched him on an unexpected level. He wondered whether she felt the same way. He wasn't ready for anything more than friendship. But he'd promised her a sunset and silence.

The sun slid beneath the water before Jacqui took a deep breath and turned to look at him. "Thank you. You were right. I did need to get out."

Liam eased his shoulders against the back of the bench. "You're welcome."

She returned the smile. "You're good company, Liam. You know when to talk and when to be silent. Not many know that one."

He looked at her. Seize the moment…

"I was wondering what you're doing Monday evening."

"Not much. Why?"

"How about coming out with me? Just as friends, nothing more," he added.

Jacqui didn't say anything. Was the glint in her eyes pleasure or fear?

"If I've said something wrong, feel free to hit me or just insist I take you home."

Something flashed in her eyes before she buried it. "No, I'd like to see you again on Monday."

Liam pushed a hand through his hair, not pursuing the flash of fear he'd seen. "Great. I'll pick you up at seven… Do you feel up to a quick game of pooh sticks before I drive you home? Because it's my turn to win."

She looked at him. "Sure. Umm…is this really a 'just friends' thing? Or is there something more to it?"

He caught his breath. In for a penny, in for a pound. "That's up to you. It could be a date," he said, watching for her reaction. "If you want. It's up to you. I mean…not a 'date' date, more of a 'two friends going out together and seeing what happens' date."

"Is there such a thing?"

Liam shrugged. "I guess there is now. We could be the first."

Jacqui smiled. "I'll think about that." She was quiet for a few moments, then seemed to come to a decision. "Monday, it is. You sure I can't persuade you to come to church tomorrow instead of going to the rugby?"

Liam nodded. "I'm sure."

6

Monday morning, Jacqui stood outside the classroom, her coat pulled up against the wind and drizzle. English weather was so fickle—hot one day and cold the next. She surveyed the playground and made notes. What this spot needed was a covered area, picnic tables, a basketball hoop and outdoor table tennis—something to entice the children outside and keep them there, no matter what the weather. A roof of some kind over the table tennis would mean they could play all year round.

She looked up as Liam's voice floated through the open window. She smiled as his voice went up and down as he spoke. He must be pacing the room she realized, as his voice varied in volume. It was intoxicating listening to him. The cadence of his melodic Irish lilt as he paced and taught captivated her. Poetry appreciation had never sounded so good.

Shaking her head, she tried to focus on the paper in front of her. Where was she? Oh, yeah, hoops and table tennis. An arbor, roses, and perhaps even a small garden they could sit in. The back of her neck prickled, and she glanced back.

Liam stood in the window watching her.

She mimed being cold by rubbing her arms. Her heart leapt as he smiled back. She held his gaze for a moment, and then turned back to her work. A warm feeling spread through her at the thought of spending the evening with him.

What is it about him that makes my heart sing? Lord, he touches me in a way that no one ever has before. And he's nothing like Vince. I don't flinch around him. I even let him hug me the other night and wasn't afraid. That's incredible. But he's not a Christian. And he seems reserved, maybe even afraid of something. Like tonight…he almost said a date then backtracked.

Her phone rang. "Hello."

"Hello Jacqui, its Eve."

"Hi, Eve. Are you wishing you were out here in the lovely drizzle rather than stuck in a nice warm, dry office? Because, if that's the case, I'm more than happy to swap jobs with you." She kept her tone light. She preferred to be out here even if it was cold and damp.

Eve laughed. "No, no, it's fine. I don't want to spoil your fun. Besides, I know how much you hate being stuck in an office. How's it going?"

"It's going really well. I'm getting a feel for the place and some great ideas. Did you just call to check up on me?"

"No. I trust you implicitly—that's why you're doing this one. The reason I called is to ask if you've heard of the Horatio Corporation."

Jacqui frowned as she thought. "No. It's not even ringing any bells. Why?"

"They've rung twice now asking for you. Maybe you're being head-hunted."

"Not likely. Can you find out about them for me—see if they've got a website? Just don't give them my number until I know a little more about them. I'll be in the office at some point tomorrow, to draw these plans up. And before you ask, no I'm not thinking of moving on."

"Miss Dorne?" Mr. Forbes appeared in her field of vision.

"I've got to go, Eve. I'll see you in the office tomorrow. Bye." She closed the phone and slid it into her pocket. "I was just coming to find you. Would you like to see what I have come up with so far?"

****

Liam arrived just after six.

Jacqui answered the door, still dressed in jeans and she promptly got flustered. "Hi...I, ummm, I'm not ready yet. I still need to change."

"I know I'm early. I'm sorry."

"Yeah, you said seven. It's only six."

"When you're with me, you're on Irish time." He laughed. "You're just fine for what I have in mind. Have you been to the steam fair yet?"

"No. It's not something I ever fancied doing on my own."

"Would you come with me? I used to go each year with Niamh before she got married. Now she'd rather go with Jared, and it's just not the same going as a threesome, or even going with Patrick. Mind you, Patrick's a workaholic—hardly ever takes a day off."

He'd never gone with Sally.

"So I'm your third choice?" Her eyes sparked and there was a hint of a teasing tone in her voice, but he wasn't sure and hesitated.

"No. For one thing you're far prettier than Patrick."

"Thank you—I think. Sure, I'll come with you. I

should change first though."

Liam shook his head. "Really you look fine. So, how did your day go?"

"Fine. Come in a sec while I find my shoes." She grabbed her trainers and sat on the floor to tie them. "Mr. Forbes liked my ideas. I'll spend tomorrow in the office to draw up the plans. I can get the plants and so on fairly fast so should be able to start on Thursday."

"Wow. You don't hang around, do you? What do you have planned?"

"That would be telling. You'll just have to wait and see like everyone else."

Liam laughed. "Fair enough."

Jacqui stood. "Right, I'm ready."

"Then let's go. Thought we'd walk as it's a nice evening and it's not far." He opened the front door for her and followed her out.

****

Jacqui had hoped Liam would hold her hand as they walked and was disappointed that he didn't.

They could hear the music from two streets away. The huge rides and shows spread out all across Victoria Park with colored lights dancing in the air.

Jacqui pulled out her purse as they reached the payment booth.

Liam's hand closed over her wrist.

"Liam?"

"I'll pay. I asked you, remember? I can't ask someone out, even on a 'just friends date', and expect her to go Dutch. Or offer to pay for us both before you say anything."

"And you bought dinner the other night. Both

dinners come to think of it."

"And? Please don't tell me you're one of those women who don't like men paying for stuff when they go out."

"It's my turn to pay for something. It has to be. Isn't that what friends do?"

"Aye, but I'm paying this time. Don't argue with me, Miss Jacqui, as no one wins an argument with me."

"Is that so?" She moved up in the queue. "Has anyone ever tried?"

"Several times, but puppy dog eyes have been known to break down my resistance on occasion."

Jacqui immediately turned puppy dog eyes on him.

His laughter was infectious.

She laughed with him.

"Fine, Miss Jacqui, you can buy the candy floss." He handed over the entrance money.

"Sounds good. You can't go to the fair and not have candy floss." She let Liam lead her inside the fairground. "So where first?"

"That will be the ghost train."

"You're kidding." She laughed. "The last time I went on one of these I was terrified."

"How old were you?"

She pulled a face. "Ten."

Liam's deep laugh sent chills running through her. "Well, there you go. That was at least nine years ago."

"More like nineteen." She put her hand over her mouth in mock shock. "Oops."

"So now I know how old you are. Come on, I'll hold your hand the whole time if you want." He slid his hand into hers.

She half expected him to comment on how cold

her hand was, but instead he just held her close. The ride was nowhere near as terrifying as she remembered. Of course that could have been because of the hand gripping hers, and the warm pleasant feeling stealing over her.

"You didn't scream." Liam joked as they got out of the ride. "I'm most disappointed. Maybe we should try the roller coaster."

"Love them."

"Then let's do it." Still holding her hand, he led her over to the huge ride.

Jacqui looked up and swallowed. It seemed so much bigger than the last one she rode. She started to have second thoughts as Liam led her to the cars. Grateful he didn't pick the first one and not willing to back down and look stupid, she climbed into the car and buckled up her harness.

The first plunge had her screaming and screwing her eyes shut tight. The second had her burying her face in Liam's leather jacket, clinging to him tightly.

Liam wrapped his arms around her, holding her close.

Only when the ride was finally over did she look up at him.

"Good grief, woman, you scream like a banshee. I think I've gone deaf," he teased as he helped her from the car. "Scarier than you thought, huh?"

"Yes, much, much scarier. Not doing it again if you paid me," she mouthed, her throat sore from all the screaming.

Liam tilted his head and cupped a hand behind his ear. "What was that? Did you say something? Because I can't hear you."

"I said yes," she mouthed again, grinning at him.

"I've gone deaf and you've lost your voice from all that screaming," Liam laughed.

She flung her arms around him, hugging him out of the blue.

He hugged her back then looked at her quizzically. "What did I do to deserve that?"

"That was for bringing me here. No one has done anything this nice in a long time."

"A nice girl like you deserves nice things. And you're not the only one having fun. Come on, you can buy me an ice cream before we go on the dodgems."

"Dodgems?"

"Sure. I'm a little bumper car, number forty-eight. I went around the corrrr… I can never remember what comes next."

"That's a skipping rhyme."

"Ah. Just as well I don't know it then. I don't skip." He kept hold of her hand as they wandered through the stalls, eating ice cream until they reached the dodgems.

Jacqui wondered if Liam had made it his mission in life to hit her car as he seemed to hit nothing else. She screamed with laugher as he went straight for car number forty-eight. He then ignored the signs and rode her tail, bumping her car every chance he got. Next they raced each other down the huge Astroslide, flying over the humps. Jacqui won every time.

When Liam suggested they go on the Arrow, she had no idea what she was letting herself in for. It wasn't too bad at first, just rocking back and forth, but its swings got longer and higher until they were hanging upside down for what seemed like forever.

She screamed, her heart racing. Her hands gripped the railing, and she hoped the harness was going to hold. Back on the ground, she stood there, panting, trying not to throw up. She glanced up to see Liam's white face a stark contrast to his dark hair and beard. "Are you OK?"

"That has to be one of the most terrifying things I have ever done in my life. Voluntarily that is." He sucked in a deep breath. "And now I feel sick."

"It was your idea."

"Was it? So it was. Well, if I ever suggest anything that stupid again, will you please…?" He broke off.

"Would I please what?" The normal completion of the phrase would be 'shoot me', but under the circumstances, that wasn't remotely funny.

"Drown me with a bucket of water," Liam finished finally. "I never want to go on one of those again."

"That makes two of us," Jacqui assured him. "So now what?"

Liam winked. "Something safer and less nauseating," he said. "Like candy floss."

"I thought you felt sick."

"Not that sick."

Jacqui bought cotton candy and let Liam drag her over to the hook-a-duck. "Oh wow, not seen one of these in years, Liam."

"I haven't done this since I last came here with Niamh. I'm out of practice. Hence my desire to do catch a duck. I may be some time."

"You'll be better than me, at any rate." She stood next to him as he handed over his money and took the rod.

He spent a small fortune before he finally hooked one of the winning ducks.

"Which prize do you want, mate?"

"Ask the lady."

"Liam…"

"Don't argue." He winked. "Choose."

Jacqui looked at the vast array of stuffed animals and finally pointed to the huge monkey dressed in a striped red and white tee shirt and blue trousers. The stall holder took it down and presented it to her.

"Oh, he's gorgeous, Liam. Thank you." She hugged him. "I shall call him Jacko. He's like the one I had when I was a kid."

He smiled and kissed her cheek, his lips sending shards of flame shooting through her. "You're welcome." He slid his hand into hers again. "Want to go down the helter-skelter?"

Jacqui tilted her head back to take in the huge tower with the slide around the outside of it. It had to be the tallest she had seen. "I haven't done that since I was ten, either."

"Then it's about time you did. I'm beginning to think you haven't lived." He dragged her and the monkey over to the slide and chased her up the dark stairs which wound up the inside of it.

Jacqui sat at the top on the course canvas mat and shoved the monkey in front of her. "After you, Jacko."

Liam snuggled up close behind her, his long legs appearing either side of hers.

She twisted her neck to look at him. "What are you doing?"

His arms snaked around her waist and pulled her back against him. "Having fun."

His breath was warm against her ear, and she shivered as goose bumps appeared on her neck. "You're mad."

Liam pushed off, laughing as they flew down the slide. They landed in a tangled heap at the bottom.

The attendant shook his head at them. "Yer lucky yer didn't get stuck, mate."

Laughing, the two of them ran off. Jacqui hadn't had this much fun in ages. She didn't know much about Liam, but she was comfortable with him. Maybe he was the one. But he wasn't a Christian. Did God have some kind of plan for him? If He did, was she wrong to hope that plan included her somewhere? If her part was simply to lead Liam back to his relationship with God, that would be enough, wouldn't it?

Liam took her on every ride at least once, until breathless, they stood in the darkness lost in each other's company.

Fairground music played, and the colored lights illuminated his face and hair. Neither spoke. There was no need for words. Their eyes met, lips smiled, fingers entwined. Even their breathing was in tune. Liam slipped his arm around her shoulders, pulling her close.

Turning her face to his, she saw the way the lights reflected in his eyes. His gaze held hers, her heart skipping a beat with the intensity of the emotions filling her. Did he feel the same way?

Liam ran a finger along her jaw and inclined his head to hers, touching foreheads. "You're beautiful. Especially when you smile." His accent seemed deeper than usual.

"Thank you. You're not bad, yourself." She could feel heat flooding her face and hoped he couldn't see the blush. "I'm sorry, did I really say that?"

"You did. So would you like to see me again?"

Her heart leapt, then fell in the same instant. "Yes, but what about Sally? She's such a huge part of you."

Liam took a deep breath. "I will always love her, but she's gone." He smiled. "How about I take you out on Wednesday, and we see how things go?"

"Sounds good. And I want to beat you at pooh sticks again."

Liam took her hand. "Surely it must be my turn to win by now?"

Jacqui laughed. "Nope."

7

Every day for the next three weeks, Liam met Jacqui after work. The check for the laptop cleared leaving him short, but he'd manage if he ate packed lunches for the rest of the term. Jacqui worked all day, including lunch, and Liam started doing his marking in his lunch hour to leave his evenings free. The only day he didn't see her was Sunday when she was at church.

She tried to get him to go with her, telling him God loved him and was waiting for him to return to Him, just like He had done with her. Liam listened and then ignored her pleas, not liking the way it made him feel. Something twisted inside him each time she spoke about God, almost as if someone were poking him with a very sharp stick, chipping away at the wall he'd erected. Nothing she said could convince him to step through the door of a church. God should have saved Sally and He hadn't.

He decided to wait another month before he booked his ticket back to Endarra and started the search for Sally's killers. Neither the local police nor the missionary organization seemed interested in hunting down the people responsible, so he would do it. Vengeance was without doubt his. Sally deserved at least that.

Or was vengeance his at all? Had it ever been?

Even as he thought that, the sharp stick inside him

poked harder, almost painfully. He noticed that he was no longer trying to deny the presence of God. He wouldn't say he was softening in his attitude as he was still mad at God, but something moved inside him. It was what Sally would call 'God dealing with him.'

He looked out of the classroom window at Jacqui in her waterproof jacket directing the work men before kneeling to plant flowers in one of the borders. She wouldn't like him charging off to kill someone. It was against a commandment. He tilted his head. If he had to choose which was more important to him, right here and now, choose between revenge and Jacqui...he'd have to say he honestly didn't know. And that floored him totally and utterly.

For nineteen months straight he'd been fueled by anger and hatred and thoughts of revenge and now? Now someone had flicked a light on in his inmost being. A small, tiny, pinprick of a light to be sure, but a light none the less. And that someone was Jacqui.

"Sir?" A voice broke through his musing, and Liam turned around to solve whatever problem had come up.

****

Saturday they spent watching the carnival floats process through the town and wandered around the carnival site, eating ice cream and hot dogs. That evening as the sun set while waiting for the fireworks, which the flyers claimed would be the best ever in the history of carnival, Liam stood next to Jacqui on the bridge in the park, sticks in their hands. Playing pooh sticks was a nightly tradition, with Jacqui so far winning every single time, no matter on which side of her he stood. They held their sticks out over the water. "All right, on three. One, two, three."

The sticks fell, and they ran to the other side.

Jacqui clapped as her stick came through first. "Yay, I win again."

He shook his head. "Me thinks the lady doth cheat."

"I am so not cheating."

Liam's hand came up to cup her face, and Jacqui caught her breath as his other arm slid around her waist.

She moved her hands to his waist, her touch so light, but centering his focus fully on her.

Her body was soft under his fingers, and as his lips brushed against hers, jolts of electricity pulsed through him. He pulled her against him, her softness melding with his firmness. Her scent filled him, and her touch reverberated through him, sending his mind spinning. He'd thought a kiss was a kiss, but this— how could it be so different?

Conscious thought left him as he deepened the kiss, possessing her, tasting her, until as the fireworks from the carnival exploded overhead, showering them with red, green and golden stars, he totally immersed himself in what she so freely gave.

When Liam broke the kiss, Jacqui leaned against him. Having her in his arms felt so right—for a few moments he'd felt whole again.

"Do fireworks always go off when you kiss someone?" she asked.

His hand slid over her back, his voice tender. "I don't know. Do you mind?"

"Not at all. It's kind of, oh I don't know…" she hesitated.

"Romantic," Liam decided. He knew how he felt, and Sally wouldn't want him alone forever.

"Yeah, I guess it is." She paused. "Does this mean we've moved on from being friends?"

Telling her was a risk, but then so was living. He'd come so close to dying that he couldn't lose anything. He ran his hands over her arms and gazed into her eyes. "I'll always be your friend, but I..." he hesitated. "I love you, Jacqui."

She looked at him, her eyes shining. "I love you too, Liam."

Liam wrapped his arms around her, and kissed her again. Maybe she was the one to fill the hole in his heart after all. This time the fireworks went off inside him, his whole body tightened, responding in a way he'd long since forgotten. But the feelings invoked were new, different and he embraced them.

After a moment, he broke off and held her gaze. "Want to come back to mine for coffee?"

He tried to read her expression, unsure if that was desire in them or not. He was so out of touch at this whole dating thing. Maybe he'd just ruined what could have been a beautiful friendship. He pushed a hand through her hair.

"No," she whispered, after a pause, her cheeks scarlet. She looked away, the words tumbling in a rush. "It's not that I don't want coffee, but I don't want to give you the wrong idea and make you think I'm saying yes to something else if I come back to yours, because I'm not. I—"

He turned her face back to his. "Hey. Don't turn away. It's fine. I didn't mean anything other than coffee, I promise. I'm not the kind of bloke who gives himself away after a couple of kisses. God and I might not be speaking right now, but my morals are intact. Some things are intended for marriage only." He kissed her forehead. "How about we go find a late night café and have coffee, then I'll take you home?"

She smiled, the relief evident in her eyes. "That sounds good. I'd like that."

"Good. Besides, I just remembered I haven't cleaned my place in a few days, and it's like a pigsty."

"It can't be that bad."

"I would have to disagree with you there. It's not as bad as it can be, but it's pretty messy. Far too messy for houseguests at any rate."

****

Break time on Monday came, and Liam went to hunt down Jacqui. He hadn't seen her for two days, and he missed her like crazy. He hadn't expected that. He'd gone from never wanting a woman other than Sally, to his heart and mind opening just a crack to Jacqui, to find her suddenly filling every waking thought. Oh, Sally was still there, too, but it was as if she were smiling at him. Pleased he was, not moving on as it was too early for that, but at least going out and having fun.

Jacqui stood over the far side of the quad. He went over to where she was standing with a clipboard in her hand, sunglasses perched on top of her head, and her hair tied back in a ponytail exposing her pretty neck to the blazing rays of the sun. She was pointing to the workmen and explaining something to them, gesturing with her free hand.

He stood until she noticed him.

"Hello, Mr. Page. Have you come to check up on

us?"

He shook his head, both of them having decided to keep things formal at school, for both their sakes. Staff fraternization wasn't frowned upon, but he wasn't ready to go public yet. "Not at all, Miss Dorne. I was wondering if I might have a word."

Jacqui gave him a dazzling smile. "Sure." She moved to one side of the quad with him. "What can I do for you?"

"Lunch," he said without preamble.

"Lunch? I thought we decided against lunchtimes, because of work."

He shrugged. "I changed my mind, so sue me. I missed you all weekend. Besides, you skip lunch far too often for my liking. It's not good for you. So, I thought you, me, and two chicken baguettes from the bakers. All topped off with ice cold soda and ice cream with a flake and sprinkles. We can get it from the van on the corner opposite the school. My treat."

"That sounds wonderful. I'd love to—" Jacqui's phone rang, and she pulled it from her belt. She frowned. "Don't recognize the number, I should take this. Excuse me a moment. I'll be right back."

Liam nodded, enjoying her smile as she answered the phone. It was a smile she reserved just for him. The call was probably a supplier. But whoever it was she'd be back with his answer. Because it sounded as if she were about to say yes without the usual haggling over whose turn it was to pay.

****

Still smiling at Liam, Jacqui wandered across the quad as she answered. "Jacqui Dorne, speaking."

"Hey, Jacqui baby, it's Vince."

Jacqui stood stock still, the lighthearted mood wiped away in an instant. How did he get her personal number? Ice filled her body, despite the warmth of the sun. She'd never wanted to see or hear from him again. He was in her past, the lid shut tight, and that's where he needed to stay. But she could do civil, she had to. Her fingers tightened on the phone when all she wanted to do was drop it and run.

Lord, please help me to be polite to him. Don't let my emotions interfere here.

"Vince, it's been a while. How are you?" Somehow she kept her voice on an even keel, adopting the tone she used for suppliers and clients.

"I'm good, hon. How are you keeping?"

The word 'hon' sent unexpected shivers of revulsion down her spine. Her reaction was a million miles away from the one he was probably hoping for. "I'm fine. So, why are you calling?"

"I missed you. Is that a crime?"

In this case, absolutely.

"No, it's not. But I've moved on." *And I haven't missed you.*

"I thought you might like an update on my career."

Not really.

"Vince, I really don't have the time—" She shook her head and called out to a sweet but inexperienced intern who seemed to like free styling the design, but this time she was grateful for the distraction. "Not there. Put it over there under the oak tree. That has to be planted in a shady area. Really, are you consulting the plans at all?" Brendan just shook his head and shrugged. "I'll be right there, Brendan. Don't dig another hole." She turned back to the phone. "Like I said, I really don't have time to chat. I have to keep an eye on this crew."

"Yes, and speaking of work, that's the reason I'm calling. There's been a company takeover, and I'm CEO now."

"Congrats on the promotion." *Just the way you like it—total control.*

"Thank you. I was sorry to hear about your parents. It must have been tough."

"It still is."

"I hope they didn't die still mad at me."

She said nothing.

"I think this whole thing has been blown out of proportion."

Blown out of proportion?

"They invested all their savings in that business, Vince. On your say so. And lost the lot."

Vince's fingers tapped, echoing down the phone. "That wasn't my fault. There were problems in Africa as well as with the finances. You know that, you were there."

"Yes, I'm well aware of that. Anyway, yes, they forgave you. They even paid my flights to get home."

"That's good. But I learned from that. I'm a changed man. So the reason—"

"Excuse me one moment." Jacqui moved over to Brendan. "Look," she said gently moving the plans through a full one-eighty degree turn. "Try it now." The light that dawned on Brendan's face would have been comical at any other time and he ambled back to the tree. She pushed a hand through her hair and sighed heavily. "I really don't have time to talk Vince."

"Ouch." His wounded tone didn't fool her for a

moment.

She turned and fixed her gaze across the quad at Liam. The concerned look she knew so well filled his eyes. She had fallen for him, despite everything.

"I have to go. Goodbye." Trying to control her anger and resentment for Vince was making her head spin.

"Wait. It took me forever to track you down, but eventually I found out you worked for the Jekyll Foundation. Then it was a matter of simply tracking you to a regional office. Where are you working at the moment? Eve wouldn't tell me."

"You spoke to Eve? Did she give you my personal number?"

"No. She gave your number to the secretary for the CEO of the Horatio Corporation. But only because my admin said it was an emergency. Your people have been putting us off for weeks."

She gave an inward grown. She'd told Eve and the others not to reply to those messages, until she knew a lot more about a company who didn't even have a website. Wait a minute, did he say *us*? All the pieces fell in place. "Then *you're* the CEO of the Horatio Corporation."

"Yes, I am."

Her heart pounded, and the edges of panic fluttered around her. Why hadn't she put two and two together sooner? Horatio *was* his middle name. "Oh, very impressive. Look, I'm really busy right now, dealing with people that don't know one end of a plan from the other, and I have to help them. Is there a reason for your call?"

"I might be able to put some business your way. Are you free for lunch?"

"No, I'm not."

"Meet me for lunch, and I'll tell you. What time do you get off work?"

"I can't. I'm too busy."

"I'm not taking no for an answer, babe. I need to see you. And you need to hear what I have to say. If only to make sure you're not holding a grudge."

Jacqui caught her breath. He had that edge to his voice. The one that meant she'd be in trouble if she said no. Not that you could say no to Vince. "Stop calling me babe." Jacqui thought fast. If he had business for Jekyll Foundation in the ever-tightening economy, perhaps she needed to listen, despite her ill feelings towards him. "I'll meet you to *discuss business*," she stressed the words. "I can meet you about twelve ten or so. Just for half an hour, no more. I'm working in Headley Cross." He didn't need to know that's where she still lived.

"Then how about Munchies on the High Street?"

"I don't have time to get there and back. There are a couple of places to eat in the precinct. I'll see you there." Jacqui hung up and stood there, hands clenching and unclenching. He'd managed to get right back under her skin. It had taken her months to get over him and now, now he was back. Well, she wasn't going there again. She'd go to lunch, hear his pitch, and then leave.

Liam took a few steps towards her and she raised a hand to stay him. She dialed Eve's number, hoping to catch her in. She left a message on Eve's answer phone, pointing out that she'd left specific instructions not to give her private phone number to *anyone* including the Horatio Corporation.

She put her phone back on her belt and took a

deep calming breath, praying hard for peace and guidance. She'd go to the phone shop in the precinct and get a new SIM card for her phone. Then she'd get the contract changed to that new number. No way was she using this number again, not now Vince had it. And she wasn't giving it to work either. Then she'd meet Vince, probably play nice and hear him out, before she said a firm no to whatever he was proposing. She'd accept whatever apology he offered and tell him to refrain from contacting her again.

Still what if this was just an act? She had to show she wasn't afraid of him, and even then knowing Vince it might not work.

Jacqui crossed back over to Liam. She hoped she looked a lot better than she felt. "I'm going to have to take a rain check on lunch. Something's come up."

"It must be a pretty big something." She could see the disappointment written on his face, conflicting with the concern still showing in his eyes and it warmed her heart.

This was new for her, having a bloke care about her, and at times she wasn't sure how to take it. One thing Vince had never done was cared about her. She had been an asset and a means to an end, nothing more. She stood there, not sure how to answer or react. She didn't want to stand Liam up. That was the last thing she wanted. But this was business.

"Is everything OK? You seemed pretty upset on the phone."

"Just something I wasn't expecting to have to deal with. He's an old acquaintance. He says he has a project he might be able to throw the Foundation's way."

"He?"

Better to be as honest as possible here. Else this relationship won't even get off the ground.

"Yes, his name's Vince Devlin. I haven't seen him for a couple of years. What about going out tonight, instead? I'll pay, make up for missing lunch."

Liam smiled. "I'm not averse to letting a woman treat me, so sure. I'll see you tonight. Pick you up about seven? Maybe we could see that film you wanted and go for a stroll afterwards."

"Sure, sounds great."

He turned to go, and then looked back over his shoulder. "You might want to put some sunblock on your neck. It's a very pretty shade of pink."

She raised a hand to her neck, the skin hot under her fingers. "Thanks. I definitely will." She watched him walk into the building, her fingers still on her neck. It wasn't just the sun making her hot. The tall, handsome Irish teacher had something to do with it, as had the one man she never wanted to see or hear from again.

The mental scars from that relationship would never fade. Neither would the physical ones.

****

The lunch bell sounded, and Liam headed out of the school. He needed to get to the building society during his lunch break. Then he'd mark the papers as he wasn't meeting Jacqui.

Who was this Vince Devlin? Someone from her past—that much was evident. Was he a school friend, work colleague, or boyfriend? He'd ask tonight. He headed first to the bank and withdrew the cash from his current account, then cut crossways across the precinct toward the building society.

There was a queue at the building society. When wasn't there? He glanced out the window. Was that Jacqui? Yes, it was. He knew her anywhere. She was standing with a tall man, blond haired, wearing a white shirt, tie, and suit trousers. No jacket, but he looked like an exec type. It must be that Vince guy.

The man slid an arm around Jacqui, then leaned in and planted a kiss on her cheek. *An old acquaintance?* One she knew well by the look of things. Had she stood him up for a date with this bloke? Was he wrong about her? She said she loved him, but maybe she didn't know her own heart. Or maybe an old flame was rekindled...

A cough made him turn back, and he moved up in the queue.

Liam paid the money into his savings account and headed back outside. He glanced around but didn't see them, so he headed back to the school. As he walked past the small Italian restaurant, he glanced in and saw Jacqui sitting opposite the man. The two of them looked very cozy. She was smiling and laughing. As Liam watched, Vince topped up her glass and knocked his against hers.

He turned away, unable to control the jealousy. He needed to get out of this relationship before either of them got hurt. He'd do the decent thing and back off, let her see this other guy. He couldn't compete with him—he probably had money and undoubtedly had a flashy car to go with the suit.

But she was special. He'd started to leave the shadows of the past behind and find happiness again. He'd been wrong—very wrong. Yes, Jacqui was special and far too good for the likes of him. She didn't need baggage like him. He was destined to be alone. The dream had been nice, but that's all it was, a dream. Any chance of love died with Sally. Besides, he had to go back to Endarra. At least now he could go back without any emotional ties.

Back at school, he ate lunch and buried himself in his marking. When class started, he taught with a ferocity and had the class busy for the entire lesson.

Looking out though the open windows he watched Jacqui plant the flowers. Her hair fell in her eyes, and she wiped the dirt from her hands on her jeans before pushing it behind her ears. As she glanced up, he turned his back and stared at the class.

With the exam group next, he'd set up the TV so they could watch a DVD of the book they were studying. That way he could shut the blinds.

His heart was breaking—again. He tried focusing on the class, and then happier times with Sally, but nothing helped. He knew what would. And as much as he didn't want to drink now... maybe if he just had one or two drinks it would help. One would be enough to take the edge off the need and help him focus on something other than Jacqui.

Once school finished, Liam drove home via the off license and bought a six pack. He hadn't taken a drink since he promised Jacqui he'd give it up, but promises were something he'd never been good at. Except one— a promise to remain faithful only unto Sally until death parted them. He'd done that—he'd remained faithful since death too. Until now, and he'd broken that with a couple of stolen kisses.

Tossing the beer on the back seat, he drove on and put the car in the garage. He unplugged the landline, turned off his mobile, and removed the batteries from the doorbell. As far as Jacqui Dorne and the rest of the world were concerned, he wasn't in. He wouldn't be very good company. It wasn't the first time he'd done this. In the early days after Sally's death, he'd hidden from the world, diving into the bottle and not coming out.

Opening the beer, he turned on the TV and flopped on the couch. He'd watch Wimbledon for the rest of the day and hope play continued well into the evening. He looked at the beer can, a battle waging within him. He liked how he felt without it, sharper, stronger...but he was alone now and without someone to help him, the will to resist wasn't there. He closed his eyes, raised the can to his lips and took a long sip.

8

Jacqui glanced at her watch again, wondering if it had stopped working. She was sure Liam said seven, and yet it was almost half past. It wasn't like Liam to be late, and after the day she had, she needed to talk to him. She tried calling his landline, but it rang and rang, and his mobile went straight to voice mail. "Hey, Liam, it's Jacqui. Are you all right? Ring me back when you get this message."

Eight o'clock came and went. This wasn't like him. Beyond worried now, she left another message on his voicemail and grabbed her bag and car keys. She had to make sure he wasn't sick or something. Outside his house, there was no sign of the car. Maybe he was in an accident on the way to meet her.

She pressed the doorbell, but she didn't hear anything, so she knocked on the door. No answer. Moving to the window, she could see the TV on in one corner of the room. He was in. She went back to the door and knocked again. "Liam?"

Still no answer. She hunkered down and opened the letter box. "Liam, please, I know you're in there. Are you all right? I don't mind not doing anything if you don't want to." She paused. "Liam?"

"I'm fine." The tight reply came through the closed door. "I want to be left alone."

"I tried ringing several times and didn't get an

answer. Are you sure you're all right?"

His shadow appeared the other side of the glass. "I'm fine." His stilted voice was tinged with anger. "I'd like you to leave."

"I don't understand. What's happened?" The figure turned away. "Liam, please, at least tell me what has upset you."

The front door flung open. He stood, tall and stiff, his eyes glinting with barely contained emotion, his lips drawn in a thin taut line and his hand shoved into his pocket. "Why should *I* tell *you* what happened? You already know. So, now you can get off my front step, get back in your car and leave me alone."

The distraught and very quiet tone he used scared her. Whatever was bothering Liam, he was upset with her. First, she wanted to know why and then maybe find a way to fix this, through prayer if nothing else was possible.

"We need to talk, but I don't think the doorstep is the best place for this, though."

"Fine," he said, still not raising his voice. "Then we'll talk in the living room."

Swallowing, she moved past him and into the hall. The door slammed shut behind her. She jumped as the sound reverberated.

Was this the right move? He seemed so angry. Maybe the wind just caught the door and blew it out of his hand.

"Second door on the right, Miss Dorne."

Her stomach sank like a stone, and she plodded in the direction he indicated. The smell of alcohol hit her as she passed him. Perhaps this was the wrong move. Too late now.

He stood between her and the exit.

Lord, help me, so I can say my bit and leave.

She hadn't been here before, and the masculinity of the room struck her as she entered. It was bare, with a minimum of furniture, the small table bearing several empty beer cans. She stood on the carpet waiting to hear whatever had sent him over the edge.

He stood in front of her, hands in his pockets, his body taut with distress as he studied her. "Well?"

"I thought we were going out tonight. You were meant to pick me up over an hour ago. I was worried when you didn't show."

"Worried now is it? You were worried. Well, there's nice." The sarcasm wasn't lost as his voice slurred.

"Yes, I was worried. You didn't call, and you didn't answer your phone. I thought you'd had an accident, but I see you've been drinking."

"The fact I didn't show up, should have given you the answer you came looking for." He paused, pointing a finger at her. "And what I do has nothing to do with you, Miss Dorne. If I want a drink after work, then I'll have one."

"What?" Jacqui looked at him. *Miss Dorne? What on earth is going on here?* "What are you talking about? What has upset you so?"

"Lunch. You could have told me. Instead, you stood me up."

"*Lunch?* Is that the problem? I told you I was meeting an acquaintance for business reasons for lunch. I even told you his name. You didn't seem to have a problem with it then. Perhaps you'd have preferred it if I'd said nothing and snuck around behind your back."

"An acquaintance who knew you very well from

what I saw. And there's no need to go sneaking off anywhere. Snuck is not a word, by the way. Least not how you're using it. It means grassed, or snitched, or told tales. You mean sneaked. Which was what you did. You sneaked."

"I'm sorry?" Jacqui couldn't keep up. "You're not making any sense, Liam."

"I saw you with him, at lunchtime. This Vince Devlin. In fact I imagine half the people in Headley Cross did." His quiet tone didn't falter. "You were flirting with him in the middle of the precinct for Uncle Tom Cobbley and all to see. Look, I get it. Old acquaintance, successful businessman, it's easy to see he's a much better—"

Anger flashed through her before she pulled it in. Yelling at him would only make this worse. "You were spying on me?"

"I was not spying on you. Why would I want to do that?"

"What were you doing, then?"

"I went to the building society to make a deposit. Figured I'd make the most of not seeing you for lunch to run some errands. What I didn't expect to see was you and this bloke looking right cozy. He had his arm around your waist, and he kissed you. Then a bit later you were laughing with him and toasting something."

Jacqui turned away. "I don't believe this. You *were* watching me."

"I was not. I told you I was running errands."

She raised an eyebrow. "Errands, really? Yet you seem to know my every move."

Liam moved over to the side and picked up his account book. He held it out to her, his fingers hiding the amount saved column. "I was in the building society, transferring money from my current account to my savings account. Check if you don't believe me. The entry is time stamped today at twelve fifteen."

She looked at him. Guilt flooded her. "OK. It's fine. You don't need to prove it. I should never have asked or doubted you."

"Why would you think I was spying on you? If you don't want to see me anymore, then at least have the common decency to tell me to my face, before doing a public display of affection in the precinct. I was a fool to even think you loved me." He paused, his tone hardening. "I think you should go now."

Her stomach twisted, and she felt sick. "Liam, please let me explain."

"I don't want to hear your excuses." He pointed to the door. "Please leave."

Jacqui reached out, not surprised when he pulled away. His eyes glittered and she wondered if that was anger mixed with the grief now. "I'm not making excuses. All I want is a chance to explain and then I'll go." She took a deep breath as he jerked his head. "You're right. Vince and I were more than old friends. We were together a long time, dated for seven years in all, but any feelings I had for him are long gone. *He* put his arm around me, and *he* kissed me. I picked at my lunch while *he* ate. I may have laughed at *his* jokes because I learned a long time ago, it's a lot easier that way. It was all him."

"I think you should go."

"Don't you even want to know what he wanted?"

"Well, from where I stood, it looked like he wants to pick things up from where he left off, and you didn't object too much."

She looked at him. If he wasn't going to listen,

then what was the point? "Fine. I'll leave." She'd said what she needed to say, she'd leave, but her traitorous heart was shattering into a million pieces.

"You do that."

Jacqui left the house, tears burning her eyes. She'd been honest from the outset, telling him she was having lunch with a guy. This wasn't her fault. She sat on the bench in the street and closed her eyes. Had her association with Vince once again managed to mess up her life? She'd finally found a wonderful bloke who seemed to care for her. Yet Liam wore his heart on his sleeve, and she could see how hurt he was because of this.

Lord? You know Vince is in my past, and. I have no desire to rekindle things with him, now or ever. Please, overrule here. I didn't intend for this to upset Liam, but it did. Right now, he feels hurt and jealous and won't listen to anything I say. I feel I should have done something to prevent him from falling off the wagon, but I know I'm only human. All things are possible for You. You can see a way where I can't. I don't want to lose what I have with Liam. Lord, please, if it's Your will, please, find a way for us to work this out. I leave it in Your hands.

****

Liam pressed his forehead against the doorframe, tears burning his eyes. Tears he wasn't going to let fall under any circumstances. How could he have let himself get sucked in like that? One day she loved him, and the next, she was sneaking behind his back with an ex-boyfriend. He didn't even know she had a boyfriend before. What other secrets was she hiding? Did she have several kids stashed away? Was she a bank robber or...

He broke off. The alcohol was wearing off, because he could see he was being ridiculous and full of blarney. Of course a woman her age would have had a boyfriend in the past. Maybe even several. It was part of growing up.

But why did it hurt so much? Normally drink dulled his emotions, this time it exacerbated them.

He peeked through the glass panel of the front door. Guilt flooded him as he saw Jacqui was sitting on a bench by the roadside. He'd asked her to explain, and then cut her off. *Idiot. Didn't even try to hear her out.* Humble pie wasn't exactly his favorite thing, but sometimes you just had to suck it up, like now. Grabbing his keys he left the house and walked down the path. He flopped down on the bench beside her, wanting to set her straight, let her know what a fool he'd been.

"Jacqui..."

"Liam." Her quiet tone held barely contained tears.

"I'm not drunk."

"Yes, you are. I can smell it. And you're not a very nice drunk either. I thought you said you were going to stop."

"I did. I have...I..." He looked down, his face burning with shame. Sally would be furious if she saw him now. And very disappointed. Just like Jacqui was. He looked up. "I'm sorry. I'd only intended to have one, but one led to another and another. And before I knew what was happening..." He sucked in a deep breath, a stale taste in his mouth. "It's not easy. They say once an alcoholic, always one. It's like there's a constant war going on inside me and sometimes the 'I need a drink' side wins and sometimes the 'Oh no you don't need one' side wins. But tonight I lost a battle."

"Yeah, you did."

"Please, look at me." Finally, she lifted her face to his. "If you want to explain, then come back inside and I promise I'll listen. I let my jealousy, and my past, get the better of me."

"You think?" Jacqui wrinkled her nose.

"OK, I know I did. I'm so sorry. Would you please come back inside so we can talk?"

I—" She paused for a long moment. "Drunks scare me. They always have."

"I'd never hurt you. But if you don't want to come back inside I understand."

She flicked her gaze at him, then looked away, as if she was considering something.

"You have to clean your teeth to get rid of the smell and throw away of all those beer cans, including any full ones you still have."

"Sure." He agreed, grateful she was giving him a chance.

Jacqui nodded. "All right. I'll sit here for ten minutes, and then come in if everything is cleaned up."

Liam stood. "I'll go put the kettle on and leave the door on the latch for you." He headed back to the house.

Would she come in?

He wouldn't blame her in the slightest if she didn't. But she'd said she would and his spirits lifted just a little.

9

Liam waited for the kettle to boil as the front door shut. "I'm in the kitchen. End of the hallway."

Footsteps echoed on the tiled floor then her shadow crossed the doorway. From the lounge came the sound of clapping from the TV. Her voice still held the echo of her tears. "Sounds like someone won. Who was playing?"

"Henson and Tyler. It was a quarter final."

"Who did you want to win?"

"Tyler, of course, he's the Brit. And before you ask, yes, he lost. As always."

She gave him a slight smile. "Bring back the glory days of the seventies."

"I still think the only reason Virginia Wade won then was for the silver jubilee." He made the coffee and handed her a cup. "We can sit in here or the other room."

Jacqui moved to the table and sat. "Here's fine."

She ran her finger around the rim of her cup.

Liam sat opposite, figuring it best to keep his distance, so she wouldn't be scared. "I really am sorry, Jacqui. I was hurt and angry."

"I know you were. But it's not like I *sneaked* around behind your back. I told you I was having lunch with an old friend. I even told you it was a bloke."

"You never mentioned he was an old boyfriend."

"I hadn't said anything about Vince because it's over. It has been for a long time. I would have told you at some point. I just didn't know how."

"Will you tell me now?"

She took a deep breath. "We met at university and went steady for a couple of years, then played it cool during his finals. He was a couple of years ahead of me. After his finals, he went into his father's business and we dated on and off. He likes his drink a little too much at times. It tends to loosen his tongue…and his hands if you know what I mean. All in all, he's a smooth operator, can talk the hind leg off a donkey, and then persuade it to walk ten miles to the river and drink. He persuaded my parents to invest all their savings into building an orphanage."

No wonder drunks scared her. Had this Vince laid hands on her? It would explain why she thought he'd hit her. "Is that the project you said you worked on overseas?"

She paused for a moment, twisting her hands on the table. "Yeah. It failed. My parents lost everything apart from the bungalow. They used the last of their money to fly me home. Dad had a heart attack, and I sold my place and moved in with them to help Mum care for him. I didn't see or hear from Vince for a few months. Then he turns up on the doorstep with a ton of money. He apologizes and asked if this would make everything all right. Would the money make up for the damage he'd caused and the losses they'd incurred? Dad forgave him. He always was the forgiving sort, and took the money. But it came with a price. Vince wanted me back. I was so grateful at the time, and he seemed to have changed, I went out with him a few times. But then he just up and left. I never looked back.

I never wanted to."

His hands covered hers, sorrow and compassion filling him. How could he ever have thought she'd be better off with this bloke? Appearances were so deceptive. "I'm sorry. Did he give a reason why?"

Color filled her face. "He went further than I wanted one night and hurt me. Dad wanted to file charges, but I stopped him."

Liam stiffened and Jacqui squeezed his hands.

"Nothing really happened. But Dad was so upset that he gave all Vince's money to charity. Anyway, when my parents died, I took over the bungalow. I've planted some new flowers in the garden and redecorated my bedroom."

The shock of her frank admission had the effect of a bucket of ice cold water, sobering him instantly. Anger and a desire to hunt this Vince Devlin down filled him. "Why didn't you file charges?"

"He didn't rape me. Nothing really happened. He just...his hands wandered a little too much. I stopped him. He slapped me. His ring cut my cheek. Then he called me frigid and left."

"Was that the last you heard of him?"

"Until today. He seems to have changed, grown up maybe, but there's nothing going on, Liam. He always was the touchy type, but if you watched for another moment, you'd have seen me threaten to deck him if he touched me again."

He held her gaze. "Seriously? You'd deck him?"

"Yeah."

"Well, that would save me doing it."

A slight smile crossed her face. "You'd do that? For me?"

"Sure I would. Women are treasures, not objects."

He smiled back. "So what did he want?"

"He's been trying to get hold of me for weeks. I thought some company was just head-hunting and ignored the calls. Eve finally gave them my mobile number, and he rang this morning at break time. I have since changed my number and not even given it to work."

"Which company?"

"The Horatio Corporation. He's the CEO."

"Never heard of them."

"Nor had I. And interestingly, they're not on the internet. No website, no email, no nothing. Another reason I wasn't going to return their calls."

"That's unusual in this day and age. I thought most business was drummed up on line now."

"Anyway, he offers me a job, heading up a project in Africa somewhere. It gets his mother's name and a plaque saying the Horatio Corporation put up the funds, and everyone's happy. He even offered me a five figure salary to do it. Not that he gave me any more details about it. He said he'd give me those once I accepted. I said I'd think about it."

"What's there to think about?"

"He's a difficult man to say no to, very charming and suave, even though I know his background. Actually, make that not so much hard to say no to, as getting him to take no for an answer. I'd rather say no over the phone, but then he'd have my number again. Aside from the fact I don't want to be anywhere near him, I have other considerations now. I have this current tender, my job and..." She raised her eyes to his. "You."

"Me?"

"If you still want me around."

Liam squeezed her hands. "Yes, if you'll have me after I so spectacularly messed up and fell off the wagon, I still want you around."

His mobile rang, and he picked it up reading at the caller ID. "Excuse me, but I have to take this. I'll be right back." He answered the call, heading from the room. "Page."

The line crackled making the voice on the other end hard to hear, but the African accent of his friend was evident. "Hey, Liam, it's Manu. I got that information you wanted."

"That's great, Manu. Thank you."

"I've emailed it to you, but I figured you'd want to know so you can check your mail."

"Thanks." He turned on the computer. "I'll check as soon as the computer boots up."

"All right, mate. Listen, I'd think twice before getting involved. Just pass this info on to the police or your contact at the missionary society. Let the experts handle this."

"Why's that?" Liam's curiosity peaked. He'd had numerous conversations with Manu about what he'd do once he traced the bad guys, and never once had Manu warned him to back off.

"This goes deeper than you realize. There's money behind this, Liam, lots of money. They ain't going to let nothing stand in their way, mate, and I mean nothing. Not you, not some need for revenge you have, not no one or nothing."

"I'll take that under advisement. I'll talk to you later." He broke the call and turned back to the computer. He started to check his email, and then stopped. If Jacqui found out, she'd leave, and he didn't want that. This could wait. He wanted...needed to finish the conversation with Jacqui first.

There was a choice to be made. And he chose Jacqui. He'd read and if need be pass on the information later. He headed back into the kitchen. "Sorry about that."

She smiled. "Old friend?"

The irony wasn't lost on him. Nor was the fact he was putting the living over the dead for the first time. "Someone I used to work with. He's been tracking down a mutual acquaintance, and he thinks he might have found him."

"Cool. Are you going to meet up?"

"I'm thinking about it. And the irony isn't lost on me. Only difference is, this bloke isn't likely to want to kiss me." *Kill me, yes, kiss me, no way.*

She laughed. "Glad to hear it."

"So am I."

"Can we try again? I promise there will be no more meetings with old boyfriends."

Liam put on a serious expression. "And I promise I have no old boyfriends waiting in the wings, either."

She laughed again. "That's a good thing."

He scrunched his nose up at her. "Or girlfriends come to that."

She took his hand. "You know, if seeing Vince again today showed me anything, it's that God was right. Vince wasn't the man for me, and it was a good thing we broke up."

"Oh?"

"Seeing him again, it reminded me of how bad things were. God does know best. I mean, if we stayed together, I wouldn't be here now with you. My parents might still be alive, but I somehow doubt that. If God wanted them to be with Him, then if it wasn't the train, it would've been some other way. At least it was quick—the coroner said they died instantly, and they couldn't have known it was coming. Knowing you is one of the best things to have happened to me in a long time."

He glanced down at her hand in his. "How is knowing a bloke like me a good thing?"

"I like being with you. I care for you a lot. You make me feel alive. Vince never did. I believe God wants us to be together. But I can't get myself into another mess like the one with Vince."

"You, what?"

"Listen, just now, back then I prayed God would intervene, and He did. He fixed the mess I made of things. Liam, I care about you and want you to get help. I know you're not convinced you need it, but there's a midweek meeting tomorrow night at the church. Come with me, listen to what Pastor Jack has to say, and maybe speak with him afterwards."

Liam pushed a hand through his hair and then rubbed the back of his neck. Now he was confused. What was she saying? Did she want to go out with him or not? He had to know and that meant asking direct, his heart in his hands as he did. "Are you telling me in a roundabout way that unless I rekindle my faith, you won't go out with me?"

Jacqui took a deep breath. "Not just that. Whatever it is that's eating you up inside, can only be solved with God's help. And I don't just mean the drinking, although He'd be able to help you with that as well."

Liam shifted on his chair, the sharp stick of his conscience once again poking him. Niamh had tried several times to jumpstart his faith over the past couple of years and he'd brushed her off every single time.

But not Jacqui. How did she manage to get under his skin? Something was changing and moving, and he wasn't sure he was ready for it.

"What's bothering me is the fact that God didn't do anything. I needed Him. Sally needed Him. I screamed for help, and He sat there, on His throne in heaven, and let those kids die. Sally died in my arms, and I had to tell her parents that their baby, the wife I promised to protect with my own life, was dead."

"I don't have the answers, which is why you need to talk to someone who might."

"I told you I'm not..."

"Then talk to Pastor Jack with me afterwards. Please, it can't hurt."

"I'll think about it."

"Thank you. That's all I ask." She flung her arms around him.

His lips found hers, and he kissed her, deepening the kiss as she parted her lips. He'd never known a woman who touched him the way she did. The kiss grew more intense, and he pulled her towards him, her body seeming to fit perfectly with his. Her hands moved over his back, through his hair, possessing him as he possessed her. After a moment, he pulled back. "I...have to stop. I'll see you tomorrow at school."

"Sounds good." She took a deep breath and stood. "Walk me to the car?"

"Sure." He took her hand, leading her outside into the darkness. "Until tomorrow." He caught her lips with his and kissed her. Finally, he let her go and stood waving as she drove away. Once her tail lights were out of sight, Liam headed back inside, going straight to the computer. He needed to know what this email said.

He watched as the info scrolled up on the screen.

His stomach twisted and plummeted. That was the one thing he hadn't expected. "You have got to be kidding me." He reached for his phone and dialed Manu. "Manu, its Liam." He started the call with no preamble at all, not wanting to waste words or time. "You're having me on, right?"

"Liam, this is not a good time, mate, and this line isn't secure."

"Just tell me one thing. Is this information one hundred percent certain?"

"Yes, now I got to go. Catch you later." The line went dead.

Liam read the e-mail again, still not wanting to believe the coincidence. Vince Devlin, CEO of the Horatio Corporation, had devised, funded, and executed the raid on the Endarra mission. The same Vince who had attacked Jacqui, had lunch with her, and offered her a job. The bloke he'd never heard of before today and was suddenly popping up everywhere. Vince was responsible for Sally's death, for him being shot, and the deaths of the others.

"Why?" Rage filled him. What possible motive could Vince have had for doing it? *Wait a minute. Vince offered Jacqui a job designing something in Africa. What if it was the Endarra mission he was planning on rebuilding?* He needed to do some digging and find out more. Typing hard and fast, he forwarded the email to his older brother. Patrick was a spook and had contacts all over the UK and abroad. Despite the numerous TV programs to the contrary, the security agencies did work together on occasions. Patrick had promised to help him as much as he could when Sally died. Everyone else had put their faith in God and the local authorities.

Liam picked up the phone. He and Patrick were adept at speaking in code. "Hey, bro," he said as the answer phone picked up. "You might want to check your personal email when you get the chance. Something came up in class regarding that school project I mentioned a couple of weeks ago. I didn't know the answer, but told the kids I knew a man who did. You know where I am. Bye."

He headed to the bathroom and got in the shower, his mind whirling. What he didn't understand was how things seemed so woven together. Was it a coincidence that the day Vince Devlin waltzed back into Jacqui's life, a whole bucket load of information implicating him in Sally's death turned up? A couple of years ago, he'd say it was the hand of God. Today, he put it down to a cruel twist of fate, irony, a fluke, happenstance as his mother would say, nothing more. He turned off the shower, dried off and got dressed.

He wasn't going to tell Jacqui. Not yet. But he had to keep her away from Vince. He wasn't going to lose another woman he cared about to the same man.

Climbing into bed, Liam caught sight of his Bible. Covered in dust, it lay on the floor under the dresser. That seemed wrong and something stirred within him. He got up and rubbed his hand over the cover. What did the song say? *When a Bible's well used, the devil's not amused?* Well, there wasn't much chance of that. He flicked through the pages slowly. He hadn't even done that much since Sally died.

It fell open in Jeremiah at a passage Sally had marked. *'For I know the plans I have for you,' declares the Lord, 'plans to prosper you and not to harm you, plans to give you hope and a future.' Yeah, right.*

He didn't doubt God was there. His problem lay

in believing in a God who would abandon His people when they needed Him the most. Perhaps God would listen to him if he went to church. He grabbed the phone and rang Jacqui's new number. He got her voice mail. "Hi, it's Liam. I wanted to let you know I'll go to church with you tomorrow. Pick me up about five thirty, and we can eat first. See you tomorrow. Goodnight."

Was he doing the right thing? He didn't know, but one thing he did know was he needed answers, and he needed to be close to Jacqui to keep her safe.

10

The church stood in the middle of a quiet residential street in the heart of the town. Its angular lines and grey and red stonework blended in with brick town houses.

Liam stared up at the familiar stained glass windows—she hadn't said it was *this* church, the one he used to go to and his whole family still attended. Hopefully his parents, Niamh or Patrick wouldn't be here tonight. He really didn't want that conversation right now.

He hadn't been inside a church since Sally's funeral. His insides churned. He wasn't scared. Scared was standing in front of a maniac with a gun who was firing point blank at you. Scared wasn't stepping foot inside a church.

Jacqui's hand slid into his, and her quiet voice filled his senses. "Are you sure you want to do this?"

"Yeah, what's the worst that can happen?"

"You discover the horrid truth about me."

He raised an eyebrow. "You're really a leprechaun?"

"No, silly. I'm actually tone deaf." She squeezed his hand. "Come on."

They found seats towards the back of the hall. Liam sat down, not letting go of her hand. "You don't use the main church?"

"Not for the midweek meeting. We use the chapel

109

on Sundays and for special church meetings. Otherwise, we meet here."

The service got underway.

Jacqui was right about being tone deaf, but that didn't matter. His mother always said it was 'make a joyful noise unto the Lord' not make a tuneful one. He listened to what was being said, finding it easy to slip back into the routine. It was comforting and familiar. He knew all the hymns and found himself singing the bass part without thinking.

He even knew the passages Pastor Jack referred to as he spoke on faith and forgiveness. Problem was, his faith was no longer there, and forgiveness wasn't in the cards. Sally's murderers didn't deserve it, and neither did he. Something inside him moved, but he refused to let the torrent of emotions sway him.

'God loves you, Liam. Just because you doubt Him, that doesn't mean He doubts you,' was what Jacqui had told him. *'He wants you back, like He wanted me back, and He wants all of us.'* After the service ended, Jacqui took him over to the kitchen to pick up coffee. He stood and sipped it, half listening to conversations around him, the other half of his mind swimming with questions and a need for something to fill the hole inside him.

Jacqui touched his hand. "Are you all right?"

He grabbed her fingers and paused for a long moment. Something compelled him to be honest. "Not really."

She led him over to a table and sat. "What's wrong?"

Liam slumped into the seat next to her and gazed into his coffee. "Where do you want me to start?"

"The beginning?"

"That would be back in the dark ages, then."

"Jacqui...how are you?" Pastor Jack spoke to Jacqui, then to him. "Nice to see you again, Liam. It's been a while."

He shook Pastor Jack's hand, managing to formulate a response. "Yeah, it has. I told Jacqui I'd come with her tonight."

"How are you? Not seen you since the funeral."

"I'm managing."

Jacqui shifted her eyes from Liam to Pastor Jack. "Pastor, have you got a minute?" Jacqui asked.

"Sure." Pastor Jack set his coffee on the table and took a seat. "How can I help?"

Jacqui squeezed Liam's hand. "Talk. It might help."

"This used to be our church." He took a deep breath. "You know the story, Pastor. Sally and I were out on the mission field in Endarra. Gunmen attacked the compound, killing most of the people there, including Sally. They burned everything. I haven't set foot in a church since her funeral—here or anywhere else."

Pastor Jack looked at him unswervingly. "Do you blame God for what happened?"

Liam caught his breath. This guy was perceptive. He hit the nail right on the head. "Yes, I do. God could have stopped the gunmen. He could have given us warning or time to get to our own guns to defend ourselves. He didn't. He let it happen. The local police are in the pockets of whoever did this because they have done nothing. The mission society hasn't either. It's like they don't care, and don't go quoting Romans chapter eight verse twenty-eight at me either."

Pastor Jack paused with the coffee at his lips. "Oh?"

"*And we know that in all things God works for the good of those who love Him, who have been called according to His purpose.*" Liam recited.

"Do you remember how that passage ends? Nothing can separate us from the love of God. Then there's first Peter chapter five, verse seven."

"If He cares that much, then prove it."

"John three, verse sixteen doesn't say 'For God so loved the world with the exception of Liam Page'."

"Now you're mocking me. Anyone can take stuff out of context. For example, Deuteronomy five, verse thirty-three is 'live long and prosper'. And this," he continued holding up his hand in the Vulcan salute, "is the sign of the priestly blessing from Numbers six, verses twenty-four to twenty-six."

"I didn't know that. I didn't mean to mock you, Liam. I was trying to make a point."

"May I?" Liam picked up Jacqui's Bible and opened it. He pushed it across the table. "Psalm eighty-eight, verse eighteen."

"*You have taken my companions and loved ones from me. The darkness is my closest friend.*" Pastor Jack skimmed the rest of the passage. "It sums up how you feel right now. How I felt after Elisa died, but He doesn't leave us in the dark. Are you familiar with the story of Job?"

"Uh huh. He lost his wife and kids, so God could prove a point to His stubborn people. Then he remarried, had more kids, and lived happily ever after." He struggled to keep his voice level.

"His wife disappeared. It's entirely possible she's the same woman he had his second family with at the end of the story, but, yes, bandits murdered his kids. Or if you prefer, terrorists."

Liam glanced down as Jacqui slid her hand into his and took a deep breath. "I see where you're going with this, Pastor, but I don't understand why. Sally hadn't done anything wrong. She wanted to teach the kids about Jesus. I went to protect her and teach the kids out there a little English. What was wrong with that?"

Pastor Jack took a deep drink of his coffee. "I don't know all the answers, and I'm not going to pretend I do. I'm not God, and I don't know why this happened and what He has in mind for you. In Jeremiah chapter twenty, Jeremiah doubted the goodness of God when he learned all of Judah was to be handed over to its enemies or killed."

"Verse nine. *If I say, 'I will not mention Him or speak anymore in His name', His word is in my heart like a fire, a fire shut up in my bones, I am weary of holding it in, indeed, I cannot*," Liam whispered. Perhaps that was the 'sharp stick' that had been poking him these past few weeks.

Pastor Jack nodded. "It's elsewhere in the Bible too. David, Hosea…even Jesus knows what it's like to be tempted, to suffer and die, and to be abandoned."

Liam straightened in the chair. "Abandoned?"

"My God, my God, why have You forsaken Me? Or if you prefer, *why* have *You* forsaken *Me*? Throughout the gospel of Mark, God proclaims His love for His Son. 'This is My Son, whom I love'. Then comes the crucifixion and there is nothing. There is no light from heaven, only darkness. There no voice from heaven, only one voice crying in great pain '*My God, my God, why have You forsaken Me*?' God has a plan for all of us, Liam, and if He delivered His own Son to death, the worst kind of death, why should He step in and save us from following our Lord's example and giving our lives for God?"

Liam's stomach lurched. "I guess... I just..."

Pastor Jack turned the Bible back a few pages, then turned it back to face Liam. "We all have doubts from time to time. Yes, even Pastors have doubts and fall into sin, but each time, Liam, like I explained earlier this evening, God still loves us. He never lets go of us, even if we let go of Him for a little while. Read Psalm seventy-three. See the big change in the middle of it, in particular when the Psalmist realized the implications of eternity. He realized that although he had doubts, God still loved him and had a plan for him. Just like He loves and has a plan for you."

Liam's hand whitened around the cup. "I begged Him to intervene, but He didn't answer."

"God always answers. The gunmen attacked, you were injured, your wife and several others died. You cried to Him for help, and you feel He ignored you because the slaughter continued. He didn't ignore you. God always answers. Sometimes the answer isn't the one we want. Sometimes the answer is not yet. Sometimes the answer is no. It doesn't mean He doesn't stop loving us."

"Why?"

"Like any child, what we want isn't always what's best for us. We may never understand while here on Earth, but one day we will."

Liam brushed a hand over his eyes and pushed up. "Thanks. I should..."

Jacqui tugged at his hand. "Don't go, Liam."

He stood still; hesitating for a moment, then shook his head. "I have to go. I'll see you tomorrow."

"Can I give you a lift?"

"No." He hurried from the building, trying to

ignore the pounding inside of him. Catching the bus home, Liam put his headphones on, blasting his MP3 player as loud as he could stand it. He didn't want to listen to the small, insistent Voice.

****

Liam continued to ignore the Voice and everything else, including his phone and email the next day. He rang in to work sick and sat on the couch, staring across at the bottle of wine he'd picked up on the way home from the church on Wednesday. He didn't remember buying it but it wasn't there when Jacqui visited on Tuesday.

He didn't know how long he stared at the bottle, before he thumbed through the phone book searching for an address.

He rang the information line and listened to the times given. The nearest meeting was just around the corner from him. If he left now he'd have time to make the start of the session. The evening sun was warm, almost too warm for seven PM. He rolled his shoulders, the familiar ache starting under the rough cotton of his shirt.

The doors stood open and he could hear muffled voices spilling onto the street. He hesitated. The Voice seemed to reverberate in his head.

Go.

Was this really such a good idea? The Voice told him so, but honestly, he'd never felt good enough for God. Not even this would do that.

God… He paused. *I'm not worthy to even speak Your name. I don't deserve the help these people can offer. I've thrown it away too many times. What do I do? How can I do this?*

Go.

The Voice was louder, but at the same time gentle and loving.

But I'm not worthy…

Go. One day at a time.

He could do that.

Making his way inside, he took one of the few remaining seats. He sat quietly, listening to the others speaking, still not sure he could do this. Then the coin passed to him. He hefted the weight in his hand and looked at it.

"Just pass the coin along the row if you don't want to say anything," the group leader said. "No one will think any the less of you."

Liam took a deep breath and slowly looked up. "My name's Liam. And I'm an alcoholic."

****

When he went back to work on Friday, he continued to block out the Voice still whispering insistently inside him. Every day. Every hour. Every minute.

"Mr. Page?" Jacqui greeted him.

"Hello, Miss Dorne. It's looking good out here. The kids love the picnic area."

She smiled. "They'll like the table tennis even more when it goes in later today. I wondered how you were. You weren't here yesterday. Have you been sick?"

"Yeah, but I'm all right now."

"That's good. I was wondering what you were doing tonight?"

Liam dodged a couple of running teenagers. "I was going to watch the tennis. Why?"

"I owe you dinner, and I was wondering if you'd let me cook for you."

He paused for a moment. He'd not had a woman cook for him since… "I'd like that. Thank you."

"All right," she shifted the clipboard in her arms. "I'll see you at my place about seven."

"Sure, see you then."

The rest of the day he spent wondering if he should take something with him. And if he did, should he take flowers or chocolates? Should he wear jeans or slacks or stay in his suit? Would she want casual or formal? He should have asked. He was so out of practice at this, despite having dated her for over a month now. He was tempted to ring Patrick and ask him, but really wanted to keep the relationship with Jacqui quiet for now. He hadn't even told Niamh, and he usually told his twin everything.

Deciding on casual, he picked a blue shirt and jeans and plumped for both flowers and chocolates. Feeling incredibly nervous as he rang the bell, he wiped his sweaty palms on his jeans, hoping he wasn't underdressed.

Jacqui answered the door in a floral sundress, her hair scraped back in an untidy ponytail. "Hi."

Liam kissed her and held out his gifts. "I didn't know what flowers you like so I got carnations." Of course he'd technically given her carnations when they first met, although he hoped these would go nowhere near her laptop.

She beamed. "You guessed perfectly. These are my favorite. Thank you. Come in."

The smell of cooking floated from the kitchen,

making his mouth water and his stomach growl in anticipation.

"The tennis match is on in the lounge. Help yourself to a drink and make yourself at home. I'll be right in with the food."

He nodded and went into the lounge. The curtains moved in the breeze. A bottle of wine and another of juice were on the sideboard. "I didn't think you drank."

"I got it for you. Unless you fancy something else." Her voice echoed down the hall.

Liam looked at it, torn and severely tempted. He could still see the look in her eyes and hear the disappointment in her voice when she found him in a drunken rage three days ago. His hand hovered for a moment, before his new found resolve kicked in. He was two days and counting. One day at a time.

He poured two glasses of juice and sipped his, glancing at the TV.

Jacqui came in with two plates. She smiled as she saw him with the juice.

"Can you get a refund on the wine?" he asked.

"I'll give it to my neighbor."

"I wouldn't want it to go to waste, but..." He paused. "I went to an AA meeting yesterday. I'm two days and counting."

Jacqui set the plates down and hugged him. "Liam, that's wonderful news."

"Thank you. Dinner smells good."

"Figured we could eat in here—slum it, as Mum used to say." She picked up the plate.

"There's nothing wrong with TV dinners every so often." He took the offered plate. "It looks wonderful. I'll swap you for some juice."

"Thank you." She exchanged the plate for the glass and sat on the couch.

Liam paused as she said grace, and then took a bite. "This is lovely. I don't remember the last home cooked meal I had."

"Thank you. It's one of Mum's recipes. Lamb cobbler—one of those 'chuck everything in the same pot' dinners, so it's really easy to do."

"Less washing up," he laughed, winking at her. "So tell me about your parents."

Liam ate as they chatted, enjoying every mouthful, almost as much as her company. She wasn't afraid around him. He carried the empty dishes to the kitchen and lost for the washing up. He picked up the tea towel. "I still think I'd have pressed charges," he said going back to the topic of her parents and an incident with the neighborhood kids.

"Dad wanted to. But Mom didn't. Despite that and everything else I did in my rebellious teenage years, my father still loved me."

Liam froze, her words hitting him right between the eyes. "Sorry?"

"I said, despite everything that happened. My father still loved...What is it?"

"Excuse me one moment." The small insistent Voice became a loud shout. Liam dropped the tea towel and ran from the room.

Locking himself in the bathroom, he leaned against the door, tears spilling down his face. *Oh, God, forgive me.* He stumbled over the words as he renewed his relationship with God and asked forgiveness for the way he'd acted since Sally's death.

He knew what he was doing and the implications. He could feel God's arms around him and His peace flowing through him as he spoke. He didn't do anything in a light-hearted way. God loved him and died for him and he needed Him back in his life.

When Liam went back into the kitchen, he felt lighter than he had for a long time. He walked back over to Jacqui and picked up the tea towel. "I'm sorry—there was just something I had to do. Some One I had to…"

She smiled at him. "I know. There's a peace in your eyes that hasn't been there before." She hugged him tightly, wet hands and all. "We love you so much."

"That's the royal 'we' I take it?"

"You bet," she laughed.

11

Liam's faith rekindled from a spark to a flame over the next two weeks. He and Jacqui read and prayed together most days. He became convinced more each day she had come into his life like this for a reason. She'd been instrumental in bringing him back to God and he was eager to see where God led them in the future. She drove him to each AA meeting and sat in the car outside while he went in alone.

He went to church on Sundays with Jacqui and to the weekday meetings. He hadn't heard from Patrick, but there was no point in hassling him. So long as he kept Jacqui away from Vince, everything would be fine, but since she hadn't heard any more from him, maybe he was finally out of her life.

The school grounds were almost done and looked fantastic. The only down side would be not seeing her at work each day.

He was due to pick Jacqui up to drive her to church. He tucked his shirt into his trousers, and then stood in front of the dressing table. He looked at the small photo of Sally he kept in with his cufflinks. His fingers traced the gold wedding ring on his left hand. "I will always love you," he told the photo. "And taking this off won't change that one iota. What I feel for Jacqui is different. I'm not sure how, but it's not the same love as I have for you, but then she's not you."

He looked at the ring and twisted it slowly until it

slid off his finger. He set it in his cufflink box on the chest of drawers in the bedroom right along with Sally's wedding and engagement rings. It felt incredibly strange not wearing it, almost like he was standing there naked, but he knew he'd never forget her. He didn't need a ring to remember her. He ran his fingers over the chain around his wrist and took a deep breath. That he'd keep wearing.

He picked Jacqui up and she did a double take at his hand. "Liam?"

"I figured it was time," he said quietly. "I'll never forget her, and she'll always have a place in my heart, but it's time. If we're doing this dating thing properly, then I need to start afresh with you, and you don't need to be made to feel second place."

"I don't. I know she's your wife and..."

"Was my wife. You're my girl now. Assuming you want to be."

She hugged him. "Yes, I do want to be your girl." She grinned. "Does this mean I get to meet your twin now?"

"You really want to?"

"Yes, I'm sure. Now come on or we'll be late."

****

Liam looked at Jacqui as the Sunday service finished. "Are you sure about this?"

She laughed. "You've been sneaking out of here for the last couple of weeks to avoid her and yes, I want to meet her. Assuming you're not ashamed of me."

"Of course I'm not. All right, she's right down there with Jared." Liam took her hand and they made their way downstairs, to where Niamh and Jared still sat in the pew talking to the people in front of them. Liam stood where he'd catch her eye, not wanting to interrupt.

Niamh's whole face lit up and tears sparkled in her eyes. "Liam." She was on her feet, her arms tightly around him, before he could react. "What are you doing here?"

He hugged her back. "The same thing as you, sis—worshipping God. I've been coming for a couple of weeks now."

"Does this mean…?" she broke off, hope in her voice.

Liam nodded. "Yeah, thanks to someone I want you and Jared to meet." He pulled Jacqui close. "This is Jacqui Dorne. Jacqui, this is my twin sister Niamh, and her husband Jared."

Jacqui shook hands with them both. "It's nice to finally meet you. Liam talks about you a lot."

"Does he? Well, he's told me nothing about you," Niamh's eyes widened as she took in his left hand. "No ring…does this mean?"

Liam looked at Jacqui and nodded. "Yeah, Jacqui's my girlfriend."

Niamh squealed and hugged him again. "What are you guys doing for lunch?"

"Not much as it happens."

"Then join us. Jarrie's cooking as he works the next four days."

"Jared's roast dinners are famous." Liam grinned at Jacqui. "You haven't lived until you try one. And he always cooks enough to feed an army. Or should that be an entire platoon of firefighters?"

"Then lunch would be lovely. Thank you."

"Follow us back to ours, then." She looked at Liam. "And you'd better not be hiding anything else from me."

Liam attempted to look innocent. "Now would I do something like that?"

"Yes," Niamh and Jacqui chorused together.

Jared laughed. "You're outgunned and outmaneuvered, mate. I'd quit while you're ahead."

Liam nodded. "Looks that way. Come on, I'm starved."

****

Liam sat with Jared on the patio listening to the girls' chatter coming through the kitchen window. "They seem to be getting on OK."

"Think Niamh's hurt you didn't say anything sooner. How long have you been seeing her?"

"I've known her a couple of months. I met her through work. I didn't tell anyone—no one at work knows we're dating, either." His fingers moved over his left hand. "Seems strange not wearing the ring. Only took it off this morning."

"Are you serious about her?"

"It's a little early to talk serious." Liam crossed his legs, going on the defensive. "That's one of the reasons I didn't mention it."

"Down boy," Jared told him. "I was just asking. Do you know anything about her? I don't want to see you get hurt on your first foray back into the dating world."

"That makes me sound like a wolf on the prowl. I'm not. We're taking things one day at a time. Her last relationship ended on a bad note—and I need to show her that not all men use their fists to solve a problem."

"That's a little hypocritical if you don't mind me saying."

Liam raised an eyebrow.

"Mr. Vengeance-is-Mine." There was a teasing hint to Jared's voice, but the jibe went deep.

"That's different. I meant hitting her. Or any woman, come to that." He noted the change of expression on Jared's face. "Yeah, her last boyfriend was a jerk of the first degree. So we're going slowly— as slowly as she needs. And speaking of women's needs, how are things between you and Ni?"

Jared shrugged. "No better. She's one stubborn woman."

"Want me to talk to her?"

"I don't think it'd make any difference, but thanks for the offer." Jared smiled and held out a hand to his wife as the women came back.

Niamh sat next to him. "Jacqui's been telling me you quit drinking, Li. Something else you didn't tell me."

Liam gripped Jacqui's hand as she sat. "I'm trying to quit. Going to the AA meetings again. It's not easy, but I'm trying. Today marks day eighteen."

"Just take one day at a time, bro." She tilted her head. "You've kept the scruffy beard."

Liam ran a hand over his chin. "It's actually tidy today. It's taken some getting used to."

"Are you keeping it?"

"Yes. At least it's not showing the grey hair yet." He looked at Jared and winked.

"That's not the reason I shave and you know it." Jared grinned.

"Don't you go quoting rules and regulations at

me. You're not in the military."

"May as well be some days with parade and full blown dress uniform. Clean shaven is one of the rules. Kind of has to be with those close fitting masks we wear. But I wouldn't change what I do any more than you would."

"Li's a born teacher," Niamh said. "More likely than not frazzled by three fifteen on a Friday, but still looking good."

"Looking good for an old man, maybe."

"Oh, get on with you. We're not that old."

"Says she who only has a birthday once every four years."

"There has to be some advantage to being born on the twenty-ninth of February."

"Of course if I didn't give her a present each year there'd be trouble." Liam told Jacqui.

Niamh playfully thumped his arm. "You bet there would. Seriously, Li, there's something different about you. I can't put my finger on it as to whether its God or Jacqui, but there is something in your eyes and in you that hasn't been there for a long time."

"Is that a good thing, Ni?"

"It's a very good thing."

Jacqui elbowed Liam. "I see a trend here—Li, Ni...it all rhymes. Do you call your brother Pi by any chance?"

Liam and Niamh burst out laughing. When Liam could finally breathe, he looked at Jacqui and nodded. "We do. However, we called him Three Point One Four for years and he never got it."

Jacqui looked confused. "Three Point One Four?"

"Three Point One Four ..." Liam rolled his eyes. "It's Pi. As in maths."

****

Niamh caught Liam's arm as they were preparing to leave. "I like her, bro," she said quietly. "You've got a good one there."

"Is Jared having a similar conversation with Jacqui?" he asked wryly.

"No, of course not. She's put a smile back on your face, and that's a good thing. Just do one thing for me."

"What's that?"

"Next time you give her flowers, don't throw them at her and especially not over the laptop."

"Am I ever going to be allowed to forget that?"

"Nope." She hugged him. "It's really good to see you, Li. Don't be a stranger, you hear?"

"I won't. I love you, sis, and I've missed you."

"Missed you, too. Now, go on and we'll see you in church in a few."

12

Liam jerked awake to the sound of the ringing. He reached out and slapped the alarm clock. The ringing didn't stop. Slowly through his sleep fuddled brain, the thought arrived that it was the doorbell. He looked at the clock twice and sighed. Maybe whoever it was would go away. The bell kept ringing. Maybe not. He got up and grabbed his robe, wrapping it around him. The bell rang again. "I'm coming."

He reached the door and flung it open, doing a double take as he saw his brother standing there. "Patrick?"

Patrick pushed past him and into the hall, his black overcoat swinging around him. He pulled off the shades and shut the door. "Did I wake you?"

Liam shook his head at his brother's abruptness. He never let himself in and never called this early. "Please come in and no you didn't wake me. I had to get up to answer the door." He yawned. "That's a silly question. It's five in the morning. Of course you did. What's up?"

Patrick put a finger over his lips and started waving an electronic gadget over the walls as he moved swiftly through the small maisonette. This was abnormal even by his standards, but Liam knew better than to interrupt. Finally Patrick put the gadget away and nodded. "OK."

"OK what? What were you searching for?"

"Bugs."

Liam did a double take. It was way too early in the morning for this. "Bugs? I cleaned yesterday."

"Electronic bugs."

He rubbed the back of his neck. "OK, you know what? Either you stop talking in riddles and tell me what's going on or—"

"Vince Devlin."

Liam was wide awake in an instant. He followed his brother as he strode down the hall to the kitchen "What about him?"

"What I want to know is how you came about the information you sent me." Patrick's cold voice sent rivers of ice down Liam's spine.

"Why?" Liam filled the kettle and set it to boil. He needed coffee. His stomach and fingers tingled. Was he finally going to find out the truth? He rubbed his hands over his face and eyed his brother expectantly. "Have you found something?"

"You came to me and sent me that email, remember?"

"That was almost three weeks ago."

"I've been busy. Talk to me, Liam. I need to know everything that you do. Who your contact is out there, what you've been doing and so on."

"I've been keeping up the search for Sally's killers. I figured someone had to—especially as the police aren't doing a thing. Three weeks ago I had a phone call and an email from my contact in Endarra. That's what I sent you. Thing is, this Vince Devlin is the ex of this girl I'm seeing, and he got in..."

"You're seeing a girl?" Patrick grabbed his left hand. "No ring. It must be serious."

"That's what Niamh said. Yeah, I have been for

almost two months. And yes I will introduce you to her. After church on Sunday if you're gonna be there."

"Should be. Back to Vince Devlin."

"Sure. The same day I get the email, this old flame of hers shows up and offers her a job in Africa, working for him, rebuilding an orphanage. He's the CEO of the Horatio Corporation, which incidentally has no website or email."

"Nice of him to look up an old flame and offer her the work."

"Not when it's the guy who slapped her around when he felt like it. And not if my suspicions are right and it's Endarra he's rebuilding."

Patrick pulled out his notepad. "What's her name?"

The kettle boiled. Liam busied himself by making coffee.

"What's that got to do with anything?"

"She could be in on this, too, for all you know. Li, your girlfriend just happens to have been involved with the man who blew up the Endarra mission and killed Sally. That is one too many coincidences even for me."

Liam scowled, tempted to throw Patrick out there and then, but he didn't. *Lord, help me keep my temper.* He settled for putting the mug on the table firmly and sitting down with his. He took a deep uneven breath before answering. "She isn't involved. I can assure you of that. I mean the guy assaulted her. He blew her parent's savings before trying to bribe them into forgiving him." He summarized badly, but got his point across. "The guy's a creep and she wants nothing to do with him. She even changed her phone number so he can't contact her again. Does that sound like she's involved?"

Patrick sipped his coffee. "Your word isn't enough, Li. I wish it were. And getting angry isn't going to help. You came to me. I'm working on it. Please help me fill in the blanks."

Liam sucked in a deep breath. "Her name's Jacqui Dorne. She works for the Jekyll Foundation. She's working at the school at the moment, redoing the grounds."

"I'll check her out." Patrick looked worried.

"So now you're interested, Pi." Liam regretted the sarcastic comment the moment it was out.

Patrick glared at him. "You're not the only one who misses her."

Liam felt a gentle tug within restrain him from the violent outburst that filled him. "I know. I'm sorry."

"I'm sorry it's taken this long. International relations work differently. We have to go through diplomatic channels, and that takes time, especially when no one cooperates. I did what I could. It wasn't enough, I know that. The evidence just wasn't there." Patrick took a deep breath. "At least we couldn't do anything officially. Not until you sent that email."

"So why did you come? What did you find out? Or is that classified?"

Patrick looked at him. "Classified, you know that. What I can tell you is that this guy has been on the radar for a while, as has his corporation. However, none of what you sent me had come up. I need the name of your contact, and I need it now."

"I can't do that."

Patrick's eyes narrowed. "Liam, you have no idea what this guy is capable of. People who cross him either vanish or die in mysterious circumstances."

"And you wonder why I can't tell you?"

"You came to me, Liam," he said. "Look, for some reason, Devlin wants your girlfriend to work for him. You know he has a history of violence as he already assaulted her once. Do I need to spell out what might happen if she turns down the job? We need to stop this guy before anything happens."

"My contact's named Manu." Liam prayed Manu would understand. He couldn't risk Jacqui's safety for anything. He picked up his phone and scrolled through it. "Here you go."

"Thanks, bro. And stay away from Devlin."

"What if he contacts Jacqui?"

"Then you call me or text me and I'll instruct you what to do. Something is going down. Can't say what, but I need you to work with me on this." Patrick looked at him. "And cancel any plans you may have to go to Endarra this summer."

Shock filled Liam. "How did you know I was—?"

Patrick raised a hand and cut him off. "I'm a spook. It's my job to know. Just do it, Liam. This is too important for you to go wandering off this summer and charging in where angels fear to tread."

"So Devlin *is* involved with Endarra."

"I didn't say that. Let me handle the investigation from now on."

Liam inclined his head slightly. "You promise you will?"

"This is *my* case now. If Devlin contacts your girlfriend, ring me immediately."

Liam pulled out his phone. "Better set up a pre-arranged code. If this guy starts following her or something, I may not be able to call you. I'll set my phone up to send you a text."

"Good thinking." Patrick nodded in approval. "Now how about some more coffee and toast before I head into the office?"

****

The phone woke Jacqui from a deep sleep. She reached out blindly to pick it up, knocking her Bible to the floor. "Hello?" Her voice sounded groggy even to her.

"Hey, babe. I'm sorry to ring so early."

"Vince?" She looked at the clock. "It's six thirty in the morning…Wait a minute. How did you get hold of my private ex-directory home phone number?"

"I had no other way of contacting you after you changed your mobile number. So I rang your office and they gave it to me on Friday."

They did what? Jacqui glared at the phone. That was something else she'd have to do today. Contact the telephone company and get a new number. Then she needed to blast whichever idiot at work gave out her home phone number.

Wait a minute. Why leave it so long to ring and why so jolly early in the morning? Oh…does that mean he's got my address as well?

Jacqui sat up and dangled her feet off the edge of the bed, sliding them into her slippers while Vince continued without as much as a pause. "I was wondering if you had made a decision about my job offer. Three weeks is ample time."

She pushed to her feet in agitation. Incorrigible didn't even begin to describe him. She walked across the room and pulled open the curtains. She leaned against the window, her back against the net curtains.

"No. I told you I have this job here, and there are other considerations as well."

"Jacqui, I need you. This job is perfect for you. You loved Africa and this gives you the chance, not to complete the one you started unfortunately, but to start something from scratch, start over. And speaking of starting over, I thought that perhaps you and I could—"

No way. Even if I weren't involved with Liam now. The mere suggestion had her swallowing hard against the sudden rush of nausea. "I'm sorry, Vince. You and I ended ages ago. Any feelings I had for you died the day you hit me."

"Jacqui, baby, listen, I'm sure we can put that unfortunate incident behind us and move on. I'm not the same person."

"Don't you dare 'baby' me, Vince. I wouldn't go out with you if you were the last man on Earth. I thought I made that perfectly clear the other week when we met. And if that didn't work, the fact I changed my number and didn't contact you should have done."

"Meet me for lunch."

Didn't he hear what I just said? "Sorry, I already have plans." She reached the kitchen and flicked on the kettle.

"Then make it dinner tonight. I really need to at least discuss this with you, one more time. I'll sweeten the deal."

She didn't bother to hide her irritation at his persistence. "Vince, which part of no don't—"

He cut her off sharply. "If you don't want to be alone with me, I'll bring Terry, you bring someone and we can all have a nice meal after we discuss the job."

Terry was Vince's second in command. A brute of a man who would do anything Vince told him to. There weren't many people who gave her the chills purely by looking at her, but Terry was one of them.

She slumped against the counter. "What's the point?"

"Just listen to the offer. That's all I ask."

"And if I still say no?"

"You won't."

Jacqui took a deep breath. There was just no arguing with this man. But she'd need back up tonight. Assuming she went at all. "If you're bringing Terry, then I'm bringing a friend."

Vince didn't miss a beat. "That's great. See you already agreed with something I said. Then we'll meet at seven o'clock at *L'espoir du Paradis* along the Riverside."

She caught her breath. *What?* That was the most expensive French restaurant in town. The chef, Pierre Garston had four Michelin stars and not only did you have to book months in advance, you needed a second mortgage just to afford the starter. "I know it. We'll see you at seven. Bye, Vince."

No sooner did she hang up the phone, than it rang again. Now what did he want? Taking a deep breath and mentally steeling herself for another onslaught, Jacqui answered the call.

"Hello?"

"Hey, gorgeous."

A smile spread over her face, relief flooding her. "Hey, Liam. How are you?"

"I'm fine. How are you?"

"A little disconcerted. After all this time, Vince just rang. Someone gave out my home number, which is actually a huge no-no anyway, but that's beside the point. Vince wants me to meet him for lunch. I said I was busy, so he insisted on dinner, with a mate of his, to discuss this job offer. I said I was bringing a friend, too. Thought maybe you..."

"Of course, goes without saying."

"If you're sure. We're to meet him at the *L'espoir du Paradis* on Riverside at seven."

"You're kidding? I'd better drag my tux out to air then. I'll drive. Want a lift this morning?"

"That would be great. Liam, something he said...the way he acted... I don't think he's changed. The way he talked...scared me."

"I'm on my way, love. Don't move until I get there. And don't open the door unless it's me." His tone lost its joviality and took on a hardness she wasn't expecting.

"Why—" The dial tone buzzed in her ear and Jacqui regarded the now dead phone in her hand in surprise. She showered and dressed and was drinking coffee by the time he arrived.

She opened the door, and he stepped into the hall, kicking the door shut. He wrapped his arms around her and kissed her, leaving her senses reeling and every nerve ending in her body tingling. When he finally pulled back for air, she smiled at him.

"Good morning to you, too. To what do I owe this pleasure?"

"Do I need a reason?" He ran a finger down her cheek and across her lips.

"No, just wondered."

"Good." He kissed her again.

Breathless when he broke the kiss, Jacqui smiled. "A girl could get used to this."

"That's the plan." Liam ran his hand though her hair. "I owe you so much, Jacqui. In fact, I was thinking, maybe we could do your Bible reading notes now, and we could read mine tonight."

She smiled. "Sure, I'll go and get them."

"Cool."

"All right, make yourself coffee, and I'll be right back."

13

That evening Liam felt like an overdressed waiter in his suit. He hated wearing a bow tie, because he couldn't fasten them if his life depended on it. Patrick had wired him up before he'd left home, making sure all the wires were hidden. He'd driven to collect her in his shirt and jacket. Jacqui had done his tie for him, a task he made difficult by kissing her while she was doing it. He could never get enough of that. If anything, his feelings for her had increased since God came into the relationship. He prayed she was the one shot he had at a second chance, and God would lead them to see it.

The restaurant towered above them. Marble steps led into it, through four ornate pillars each crowned with intricate carved pomegranates and lotus flowers. Two huge angels carrying scrolls and angled spotlights hung either side of the golden slanted letters spelling out *L'espoir du Paradis*.

He glanced down at himself. Was he underdressed? Maybe he should have worn his tux after all, along with cummerbund and pleated shirt. Jacqui on the other hand looked perfect. Her long pale blue evening dress, lace cream shawl, and pearl necklace and earrings, made her look as if she were going on to the West End theater after eating or to a red carpet film premiere.

His heart burst with pride looking at her. From the

way she moved restlessly, her hand white in his, he knew she was scared, but her outward demeanor belied it. He squeezed her hand as they waited for Vince and his sidekick to turn up. "So what's this Vince like?"

"Still a creep of the first degree." Jacqui's smile didn't touch her eyes as she spoke. "He'd sell his own grandmother in order to get what he wanted." She paused. "You know, when he rang this morning, he even asked me if I'd go out with him."

"We *are* going out with him."

She smacked his shoulder. "You know, you can be thick at times. No, I mean *go out* with him, as in girlfriend."

"Oh." Liam's face and stomach fell.

"Don't worry. I told him no way, not if he were the last man on the face of the planet." She kissed Liam. "I'm totally over him and thoroughly in love with you."

"Just as long as it stays that way."

"Yep."

"Good, because I'm rather fond of you, too."

Jacqui pretended to pout. "Just rather fond?"

Liam smiled. "More than fond, you know that. Just don't want to rush in to anything."

Her eyes lit. "I know. It's fine." Her smile froze as she stared over his shoulder.

Liam turned and followed her gaze. "That's Vince I assume. Who's that with him?"

"Terry, the closest thing to a brother the bloke has. Terry gives me the creeps, too."

"I've seen him before." *But where?* The two men approached, and Liam tried to work out where he'd seen Terry.

Jacqui held out a hand to Vince, flinching as he grabbed it and pressed it to his lips. "Vince, may I introduce Liam Page, my boyfriend. Darling, this is Vince Devlin, the old friend I told you about—my ex."

Liam held out a hand, stifling a grin as Vince dropped Jacqui's hand as if it burned him. Vince's grip was firm and reminded him of a snake. He smiled like one too. "Mr. Devlin."

Vince inclined his head. "Mr. Page. This is my business associate, Terry Willis."

Liam shook his hand. The handshake was cold, clinical, slimy and yet familiar all at the same time. Where had he met him?

"Shall we?" Vince swept into the restaurant and spoke to the maître d'.

The inside was just as highly decorated as Liam had imagined. More pillars stood against the walls, golden crowns engraved across the top of each. Angels stood guard in the four corners of the room. His feet sank into the rich red carpet, treading the gold leaves woven in an intricate pattern. Red curtains lined the windows and deep crimson paper on the walls gave the entire building a sense of opulence and luxury.

Liam wrapped an arm around Jacqui's waist as they followed the two men across to their table. He leaned towards her ear. "You didn't tell me Vince was a viper."

Her voice was just as low. "Would you have come if I had?"

"Of course I would." He raised her fingers to his mouth and nibbled them. "If anyone bites you, it'll be me. Not Vince the Viper."

She laughed. "You're a twit, but Vince the Viper describes him to a tee."

"But a nice twit, I hope. Wish I knew where I'd seen this other man before."

"He and Vince are joined at the hip." She sat down as he pulled the chair out for her and then tucked her in. She glanced across the room. "There are lots of security people over there. Must be someone important in tonight."

Liam followed her gaze. He lowered his voice brushing against her ear. "They said something on the news about a foreign dignitary visiting or something. But I thought that was London, not here."

He dropped a kiss on her neck before sitting beside her. He picked up the menu and pretended to study it while glancing around the room. Patrick and a woman he didn't recognize sat at the next table, laughing and joking. He didn't know how they'd got a reservation, but assumed Patrick had pulled his national security strings. In any event he was just pleased to see them there and he was glad Jacqui hadn't met him yet.

As instructed, Liam didn't attempt to make eye contact. His fingers brushed over his collar for an instant where the mic was hidden, then he turned to Jacqui and smiled.

Vince looked at Jacqui. "When you said you'd bring someone, I thought you meant a woman for Terry to chat to."

Jacqui laughed slightly. "I figured it'd be best if Liam came. After all this is a business dinner isn't it? Any decision I make affects him just as much as me. And I'd only discuss it with him first anyway."

"So how long have you two been seeing each other?" Vince asked.

"A couple of months," Liam answered.

"Will it bother you when she comes to work for me in Africa?"

"When?" Jacqui shook her head at him. "You mean *if* I come and work for you. I have told you 'no' at least once. Regardless, if I were to consider your offer, it would be after a conversation with Liam and praying about it long and hard."

Vince rolled his eyes. "I see. You're still on your religious kick then."

"It's not a religious kick, Vince, but yes I'm devoted to God and His will."

He smirked. "So she's holding out on you, too, Mr. Page. I have never known a tease like her."

Liam met Vince's gaze. "That's really none of your business."

Vince laughed, a cold, harsh sound that made Liam want to whisk Jacqui away from this man and to safety, but if what was discussed in this meeting lead to Devlin's arrest, it was worth it to stay.

"She tried that line on me, too. Good to know it wasn't just me." He turned to Jacqui. "My offer is still on, and the pre-nuptial agreement just needs your signature."

"I beg your pardon?" Jacqui looked at him outraged, her whole body stiffening.

Vince leaned across the table. "I'm sure I can win you over if I apologize enough. I just don't like being teased and led on. It's humiliating. But that's no reason for us not to start again." His hand ran over her arm.

Liam caught his breath, fury filling him. It was all he could do not to get up and hit Vince so hard he ended up in the middle of next week. But if Vince was involved in the bombing at the mission, then he was a dangerous man. He didn't want this man anywhere near Jacqui, therefore he'd help Patrick in any way he could. Like sitting here long enough for them to get a recording from the wire Patrick had put on him.

Jacqui pushed her chair back and stood. "I've heard enough."

"Sit down," Vince told her. "I'm just teasing. Do you want to hear about this amazing job offer or not?"

Liam tugged at her hand, relieved when she sat down again. The conversation halted as the waiter came, took their orders, and then brought the drinks over. Vince ordered a bottle of red wine and insisted on the waiter filling their glasses.

"That's a waste," Jacqui told him. "We won't drink it."

"You might change your mind."

"Don't bank on it. So, this job?"

Vince picked up his glass. "Last time we spoke, I mentioned a five figure salary, and you get to design the whole thing. You'll have a staff of fifty under you to bring your designs to life. This project is just the start. I want you in as chief landscape architect, Jacqui. The world will be your oyster. Your designs will be everywhere."

Liam took a deep breath and signaled the waiter. He came immediately. "Can I have two glasses of cold water please?"

Jacqui was still eyeing Vince. "What's the catch?"

"No catch. This first one is right up your street. We're building an orphanage on the site of a mission complex. The phoenix rising from the ashes. Sad story, gunmen raided it coming up on two years ago, destroying both it and the missionaries in it."

Liam stiffened, and Jacqui slid her hand onto his leg under the table. She managed to keep her voice level. "Is it safe to build there?"

"Would I be building there if it weren't?"

"But if the gunmen were never caught..." Liam broke in. *Surely it's not the same one. Please let this be me putting two and two together and making seven.*

The waiter came over with the water. Jacqui smiled at Liam. "Thank you."

Vince took a long drink, his eyes never leaving Liam's face, and set the glass down as the waiter left. "They were caught. My company owns the land and leased it to the mission society. I conducted the investigation along with the local police. The local authorities found and dealt with the gunmen. Terry was out there last week."

"Out where?" Jacqui asked. "After all, if you're sending me to Africa, it's only fair I know whereabouts in Africa. It's a pretty big place."

Vince smiled at her. "Endarra."

Liam's stomach roiled. He picked up his water, struggling to contain his emotions. He could feel Vince's gaze on him and didn't want him to see how the conversation was affecting him.

Vince continued speaking. "And now my investigation is complete, I'm going to rebuild the *Matumaini* mission." He paused. "Mr. Page, are you feeling all right?"

Liam nodded slightly, the nausea growing as the food arrived. "I'm fine." As much as he wanted to leave, he didn't dare. Jacqui would be alone with these men. He took a few deep breaths, praying hard as he did. Picking up his fork, he realized Jacqui was speaking to him. "It's been a long day," he assured her, working out what she said from the concern on her face.

Vince turned his cold hard eyes on him. "What do you do?"

"I teach English."

"You ever taught abroad?" Terry asked.

Liam paused with the fork partway to his mouth. "Why do you ask?"

"I'm just trying to figure out if we ever crossed paths before." Terry studied him. "Or maybe you just have one of those familiar faces."

"I taught English in a French school for a couple of years, but that was a while ago."

Terry immediately switched to French. "*Alors, vous parlez français?*"

"*Naturellement, parfaitement.*" Liam was grateful he was fluent in several languages.

"*On dit que c'est la langue la plus romantique au monde.*"

Liam laughed. "*Mae nhwn dweud hefyd mae Cymraeg yw iaith y nefoedd.*"

Jacqui glanced up from her meal. "I'm sorry, that sounds like double Dutch to me."

"It's Welsh. I said, they also say that Welsh is the language of heaven."

"Guess I better learn Welsh then." She laughed. "When did you become multi-lingual?"

"One of the schools I worked in." Liam didn't want to give too much away. He had this pressing feeling that he needed to keep quiet about his involvement in Endarra, especially in light of what Vince had just said.

Vince sneered at him. "You get around."

Liam felt the need to keep quiet grow. He had to change the subject. "So tell me about your corporation."

The conversation moved on, and Liam held Jacqui's hand under the table as he listened to Vince speak while they ate the fine haute French cuisine that well deserved its four stars. Jacqui had told him most of what Vince was saying, so there was nothing new here. His disquiet increased, a heaviness settling over him.

Lord, is this feeling from you? Something isn't right here, and I have this overwhelming desire to leave before he connects me with Endarra. He looked at Jacqui and then at his watch.

Jacqui nodded and put her fork down as she finished. "The meal was wonderful. I'm sorry to have to cut this short, Vince, but I'm expecting a phone call at ten."

Vince's face darkened. "They can always ring back."

"My friend's ringing from Australia. We worked together some years ago and kept in touch when she emigrated. We have to take the time difference into consideration." She bent down and picked up her bag. Sophie was going to call sometime this week and she always called at ten. "Thank you for dinner. I'll be in touch about the job."

Vince reached over and grabbed her arm. "I'll take you home. We can finish talking on the way."

Jacqui shook her head. "Liam will take me."

Vince shook his head. "I insist."

Liam looked at him. "Thank you for the offer, but I have it covered. I just need to go and wash my hands, hon."

Jacqui smiled. "I'll wait here."

Liam shook his head slightly.

"I'll be fine."

He stood and headed to the men's room, aware of both Terry and Patrick following him, while Patrick's companion remained covertly on alert beside Jacqui. Patrick moved into a stall and shut the door as Liam turned on the hot tap and held his hands underneath it. Terry crossed the room to stand behind him.

Liam looked up. "Do you want something?"

"I want to give you a word of advice. Don't stand in Vince's way."

Liam let the water run over his hands not bothering to look at the man. "That sounds like a threat."

"Nothing of the sort. Just a word to the wise. Vince and your girlfriend have a past he'd like to, shall we say, rekindle. This job is just the start. Vince would like you to back off and leave the decision for the lady."

Liam turned off the taps and swung around. "You can tell Mr. Devlin that I have no intentions of stopping Jacqui from doing anything. I'm her boyfriend, not her lord and master or her keeper. If she wants to stay here, that's fine. If she wants to go to Africa, then that's fine too." He pulled down a paper towel and started drying his hands.

"Does your wife know you're carrying on with another woman?"

"I don't have a wife." Liam told him sharply, wondering how he knew. With no wedding ring there was no outward sign, and they certainly hadn't discussed the topic over dinner.

Terry nodded. "My condolences."

Liam jerked his head. "I should go. Jacqui will be wondering where I—"

The breath was knocked from his lungs in a gush as a fist connected with his stomach. Another blow caught the right side of his face, sending him crashing to the floor. Several kicks to his stomach and side doubled him over. He gasped in pain, holding his hands up to protect himself.

The toilet flushed and the stall door unlocked. A rough hand jerked Liam to his feet as Patrick's voice echoed in the small room. "Is everything all right."

Terry nodded. "This gentleman slipped. I was just helping him up."

Liam pulled in a deep breath and winced. "I'm fine. I should go." He took an unsteady step to the door, clutching his stomach with one hand. Patrick moved to the sink, blocking Terry's exit. Once in the corridor, Liam straightened and headed back to Jacqui. He wasn't going to breathe a word of this to her, or let on he was hurt. He knew now he had to get her away from this place and fast. He reached the table, just as Vince was escorting Jacqui towards the door.

Vince scowled at him. "I thought you'd gone without her. I was going to drive her home so she didn't miss this *very important phone call*."

Liam hissed in a deep breath and offered Jacqui his hand. "Well I'm here now. Let's go."

Jacqui took his hand. "Sure. Goodbye, Vince. Sorry to cut it short, but I'll let you know my final decision in the next day or so."

Liam escorted Jacqui outside. "I won't have you home in time for ten. You know that, right?"

"That's fine. I don't know if Sophie will call tonight or not, but Someone told me to get out of there."

"Yeah, me, too. In more ways than one."

"Are you all right?"

"Shh, in here." He pulled her into the shadows as

Vince left the restaurant alone. The hairs on the back of his neck stood up, and he pulled out his phone. The same feeling he had all evening came over him again. They were in danger here.

He speed dialed Patrick. "Patrick, it's me. Get out of there. Don't argue, bro. Please, just do it."

"Leaving now."

"We have to go." Liam held Jacqui's hand tightly as he pulled her towards the car park, walking as fast as he could, determined to get her to safety. He glanced back to see Patrick and his female companion leave, and relief flooded him. They crossed the bridge over the river, leading to the car park.

A massive explosion rocked the earth. Flames lit up the night sky. The shockwave reverberated around the quiet town center, flooding the area with a wave of light and heat.

Jacqui screamed.

Liam pushed her to the ground, shielding her body with his as the heat from the flames engulfed him. *Not again, God…not again…*

14

As the blast wave passed, Jacqui gazed into the dark eyes a few centimeters above hers. Her heart thudded in her chest, and she wondered for a brief moment if she were dead. She drew in a shuddering breath, her ears ringing. Liam's body lay prone over hers, his face creased in pain. He rolled off her. Jacqui lay there shaking. *What just happened? How did Liam get hurt?*

"Jacqui, are you all right?" She could see his lips moving, but his voice was so quiet she could barely hear him.

"Was...was...that an explosion?" Jacqui could hear the tremble in her voice. "Did the restaurant...? Those people..."

He pulled her up and wrapped his arms tightly around her.

"Are you all right?" he repeated.

"Yeah, I think so."

She tightened her grip on his hand as they gazed at the scene across the river. Flame and smoke engulfed the restaurant, billowing out from it in an inferno. She could feel the heat burning her face from where she stood.

Running footsteps crossed over to them, causing both of them to turn around. "Liam, are you both all right?" A tall, dark-haired man came up behind them.

"We're fine, Patrick."

"Good. I've called it in. The fire department is on its way. Go home."

"Did everyone get out?"

"I don't know. I pulled the fire alarm in the foyer after you called." Patrick's expression was tight. "Go home."

"Sure?"

"Yeah, just go home."

"Liam, what's going on?"

"This is my brother, Patrick. Patrick, this is Jacqui."

"Brother? You were here?" Her mind was still dazed, and Liam had to support most of her weight.

Patrick held out a hand, and she shook it as he spoke. "Nice to meet you. Sorry I can't stop and chat. Liam, take her home, and I'll come take statements in the morning, all right?"

"Sure, bro. Night."

Jacqui leaned into Liam as he wrapped his arm around her tightly. The wail of sirens filled the air as emergency crews from across the town began to respond. She walked quietly with him up the stairs to where he had parked the car. She got in and leaned against the window as Liam drove. She was shaking and couldn't stop. *Thank You, Lord,* flowed through her mind over and over in what was almost a litany. If she hadn't had that feeling, if something hadn't told her to leave, she'd be dead right now. They both would be. She had more questions than answers. Was this Patrick a cop? What was he doing there? Was it a coincidence or something more?

Liam pulled up outside his house. "Come on," he said helping her from the car.

She looked at the house and then at him. "This

isn't my place."

"I know. I don't think you should be home alone tonight. You can stay at mine."

"Liam, I'm fine, just a little shaken."

"Just humor me, love, please?"

"Just for a while." She let him lead her inside, and she watched as he deadlocked the door. His movements were small and deliberate, and he held himself stiffly. "Are you all right?"

Liam headed down the hallway to the kitchen. "I'm fine."

Not believing him for a second, Jacqui put her bag by the door and followed him. She leaned against the worktop.

"I fancy some cocoa. Would you like some?"

"Cocoa? Liam, we almost died back there, and you're going to stand there and make cocoa as if nothing happened."

He glanced at her, and her heart dropped at the bottled up emotion in his face and eyes. She moved to him and wrapped her arms around his waist. "I've got you."

His body stiffened and was that a gasp of pain he gave? Before she could ask him, his lips found hers, and Jacqui found herself drowning in the need she felt for him. She returned the kiss, needing the comfort he offered as much as he seemed to need hers. She pulled away after a few moments, breathless.

"Please, stay," he said. "I'd feel better if you stayed here tonight."

"You have a spare room I assume?"

"No, I'll change the sheets on the bed, and you can have my room. I'll sleep on the couch."

"Are you sure?"

"Yeah. Now do you want cocoa?"

"Cocoa would be wonderful. Thank you." She looked at him long and hard. "You're hurt. Was it the explosion?"

"No." He winced as he lifted the milk from the fridge.

"OK, mister, shirt off and let me see." She turned to pick up the first aid kit from the shelf over the kitchen counter. She could hear clothes rustle behind her and when she turned, Liam stood shirtless before her. His lean, muscled torso was covered with red marks. Was that a boot mark? Her eyes focused on the long jagged scar on his shoulder. She wondered how he'd got it, but wasn't going to ask. Now wasn't the time or place.

She couldn't help the gasp. "Liam…"

He shrugged. "It'll be pretty in the morning."

"Sit." She grabbed the roll of kitchen towel and rinsed several sheets under the cold tap. "Hold that over your eye." She rinsed another and started doing what she could to the bruises forming on his chest. "What happened?"

"Terry warned me off," he said wryly. "If Pi hadn't been there, I'd be toast." He gasped in pain. "Literally."

"I'm sorry. I'm being as gentle as I can."

"I know."

"Do you have any witch hazel or arnica cream?"

"Both are in the bathroom cabinet."

Jacqui went to find them and then finished patching him up. His skin was smooth under her hands as she applied the cream. She shook her head, trying to ignore the feelings coursing through her. Her nerve endings were on fire by the time she finished.

"You can put your shirt on now." She washed her hands. By the time she turned around Liam was dressed.

"Thank you. Now, where were we?" Liam said as he tugged his shirt down.

"Cocoa."

"Ah, yes. Cocoa and maybe I'll tell you a story about the leprechauns while we drink it."

****

Lying in Liam's bed an hour later, Jacqui stared up at the unfamiliar ceiling trying to make sense of everything. He'd lent her a pair of pajamas. The shirt reached her knees and fortunately the trousers had a drawstring waist otherwise they'd never stay on. Her dress would never recover. The soot and smell of smoke might come out if she had it dry cleaned, but the tears in it would never be hidden, even with the best invisible mending she could do.

She took a deep breath, taking in the lingering scent of the aftershave. Liam must have put it on before taking her to dinner. That seemed like a life time ago. So much had happened since then. Once Liam had left her and Vince alone at the table, Vince had changed. He'd gone from polite business man to full on creep and, although the threat of physical violence hadn't been spoken aloud, it was there just under the surface.

Liam had reappeared in just the nick of time, as the only way to avoid leaving with Vince would have been to have screamed and made a scene. *Terry warned me off.* She heard Liam's words in her mind again. What did he mean? Was Vince so determined to get her back that he'd remove Liam by force? Was there a connection to this blast and the one in Endarra?

She turned over onto her side.

Liam was two doors down, and she could tell by the sound of his footfalls he was pacing every few minutes. He wasn't sleeping, either.

She glanced around the room. It was so him. Just like the rest of the place, he had furnished his bedroom with the bare essentials, no pictures or photos. Strange, for a man who had such a wonderful family, not to have pictures of them on display. There wasn't even one of his twin sister, or of his wife, save the one. Plus there were none of her touches to the place, either. Perhaps he'd moved her after her death.

She ran her hands over the crisp, clean, beige cotton sheets, trying to still the agitation in her mind. The dark brown pillow cases and quilt cover bore signs of having been ironed. She never ironed anything if she could avoid it.

An hour later, Liam was still pacing, and she still couldn't sleep.

Jacqui got up and pulled on Liam's robe, wrapping it around her. She padded through the dark hall to the lounge and tapped on the door. "Liam?"

"Come in."

"Can't you sleep, either?"

Liam stood by the window. The orange glow of the fire still rose on the horizon. He shook his head. "No, my mind just keeps going over and over what happened tonight. I thought I might put a movie on to watch—something nonviolent just to help me relax a little. Or at least try to. There must be something on one of the movie channels. If not there's always the cooking or shopping channels. Would you like to join me?"

"I'd like that. Thank you."

She walked over and sat on the couch. Liam sat next to her and spread a blanket over the both of them. He picked up the remote, turning on the TV. Flicking through the movie channels, he found one they both wanted to watch. He put his arm around her, and Jacqui laid her head on his shoulder. Twenty minutes passed, and she glanced up at him as his breathing changed, and his grip on her relaxed. "Liam?"

Not getting an answer she guessed he was sleeping. She leaned against him and turned her attention to the film.

****

Liam woke at four AM. His stomach hurt, and it felt like a whopper of a bruise forming on his face. The birds were welcoming the dawn at full volume, and his arm was stiff. For a moment, he sat there wondering why he fell asleep in the lounge with the TV on, then he became aware of soft breaths on his chest. Lowering his gaze, he saw Jacqui sleeping soundly. He smiled and muted the TV. He closed his eyes again, listening to the dawn chorus.

Just after five, he flicked the TV news on and sat watching it. The fire was all over the local and national news, the death toll standing at fifteen, with several more in the hospital. The official word was a gas leak. But Liam recognized the man in the next news item as having been at the restaurant—right alongside all the additional security. The *Endarran* vice president was there? Coincidence? He didn't think so. OK, they hadn't said he was in Headley Cross, but Liam knew what he'd seen. Things were starting to add up and he didn't like it.

Jacqui stirred in his arms and opened her eyes. He smiled down at her and kissed her forehead. "Good morning, love."

She smiled at him. "Morning. That sure is a lovely black eye you have there. How's the rest of you doing?"

"Sore, I won't know until I get up and look, but the arnica cream will have brought all the bruises out overnight." He ran a hand down her face, touched by the concern in her eyes. "Don't worry yourself over me, love. I'm all right."

"What time is it?"

"Just gone five in the morning."

"How long have you been awake?"

Liam smiled. "An hour or so. I didn't want to disturb you by moving. I got woken by the birds."

"They can be rather noisy, but I love listening to them."

"I do, too, but not at five AM after hardly any sleep."

She shook her head. "You realize it'll get noisier in a bit."

He raised an eyebrow. "Huh?"

"Dawn is going to crack. With a very loud crack. You don't want to miss that."

"What are you wittering about?"

"Day is going to break, and in around fifteen hours or so, night will fall, probably with a loud bang when it lands."

He groaned. "That's terrible." He pulled the blanket over his head. "I have to be up in two hours to tell the king the sky is falling."

Jacqui laughed and pulled the blanket down. "Fine, you do that."

"I apologize for falling asleep on you like that."

"I think I was the one who used you as a pillow, but its fine. You were tired. I don't even remember falling asleep."

"I remember being really tired and thinking I'll shut my eyes for a minute, but that was it."

She nodded, her attention caught by the TV. "Have they mentioned the fire?"

"They have. They've had film coverage and everything. It made the national news. Fifteen people dead, with several more in the hospital, including a couple of firefighters."

"Fifteen?" Her tone was stricken.

"They're saying it was a gas leak." He felt her stiffen in his arms. "We were lucky we got out when we did."

"Luck had nothing to do with it. God got us out of there." She paused. "What about your brother-in-law, Jared? Isn't he a firefighter?"

"Yeah, he is. I rang Niamh after you went to bed last night. Jared isn't working nights right now—he's on days. He'll probably be there after shift change today."

"That's good. I have another question though, Liam."

"Go for it."

"Your brother said he was coming back for statements. Is he a cop?"

"Kind of. He's security services. He works for the government. He's MI5."

Jacqui raised an eyebrow. "A spook? Was he working last night?"

"How am I meant to know that?"

"You're not a very good liar."

Liam took a deep breath. "All right, yes, he was working. I asked him to check out Vince and to be there last night."

Jacqui pulled out of his arms. She got up and moved away, wrapping her arms around her middle. "I thought we were past this jealousy of yours."

"Jacqui, please, love, it's not what you think." He got up and moved over to her, taking gentle hold of her arms.

She fixed her eyes on him. "Then why?"

"Let me make some coffee, and I'll tell you."

"All right."

He let go of her and headed to the kitchen. Once she knew, she wouldn't want anything more to do with him. He knew that, but after last night, she had to know the truth. Or at least know what he did. Liam put the kettle on to boil and ran his hands through his hair.

"Well?" Her voice came from behind him.

"I told you about Endarra and watching Sally die. I made a promise that those responsible for her death would pay. I've been saving for months. That money in the building society is to fund my trip back there, to hunt down the men that killed my wife, my friends, and the kids we were caring for. The plan—once term finishes next week, and assuming I could get a flight, was to kill the men who killed the people I cared about."

"Liam." Her shocked gasp hit him hard. "Vince said..."

"He lied, Jacqui. The police did nothing. The missionary society did nothing. They didn't catch or hold anyone accountable for this. I had someone investigating. The day you met Vince was the day I heard from my contact. He sent me an email proving that Vince was responsible for the attack. He wanted the mission gone, so he could use the land himself. I passed the information on to Patrick, and he's spent the last few weeks looking into what I sent him."

Jacqui turned, her face pale and her hand covering her mouth. "I don't believe this."

"I'm sorry. I wish there were some other way to say this, but there isn't."

"You lied to me."

"I didn't." Outrage filled him. "I'm not the one in the wrong here."

"Lied by omission, Liam. You knew how dangerous he was, and you didn't tell me." She drew in a deep breath.

"Would you have gone if I had told you?"

She didn't answer him.

"Would you?" he insisted. "You said yourself, love; he's a hard man to say no to. The last thing you said to him was you'd consider an offer you'd already turned down. At least twice if not three times."

Jacqui twisted her hair into a hair band, tying it back. "I don't know. Probably, like you said he's a hard man to turn down. So why was your brother there last night?"

"Like I said, he was looking into the information I'd given him." Liam looked at her. "Yesterday morning he came over. He told me to stay away from Vince, but if he contacted you to let him know. He insisted on being there last night, wired me before I picked you up, so they could record the conversation."

She tilted her head. "But you weren't wearing a

wire last night when I patched you up. And even when I did your bow tie, I didn't see one."

"Patrick hid the wire well. Besides, I was already dressed and my collar already done up when I got to you." Liam pulled the wiretap from the bread bin. "You turned your back on me to find the first aid kit when I stripped. I had time to hide it." He paused. "Terry followed me to the gents last night. He warned me to stay away from you. He hammered the point home so to speak. Fortunately Patrick was there and stepped in. I thought the plan was to leave me there when the place blew."

"He does hammer his point home very well. He must have been a boxer at one point."

"Or a bouncer. But, thanks to your expert ministration, it's nothing I can't cope with—I've had worse."

"I don't think I want to know."

He smiled, lopsidedly at her. "No, you don't, but it's evident that Vince and his cronies don't want me around."

Jacqui nodded. "You don't think it was just a gas leak?"

"No, I'm betting there was a plan. I think you were part of it somehow."

"Blowing up a restaurant to kill you is a little excessive, don't you think?"

Liam made the coffee and slid one across the counter to her. "They didn't know I was going to be there. Vince was surprised when I turned up. Apparently that was already in play when we got there. Remember that VIP and all those security personnel?"

"What about them?"

"He was on the news too—of course no mention of him having been anywhere near that restaurant or Headley Cross last night. He's the Endarran vice president. I'm thinking he was the original target. I was just an added bonus because I can link them directly with the attack on the mission. They know that. Also, I'm standing between you and him."

"There is no me and him. There hasn't been for years."

"That's not the point."

"No, the point is you've known for three weeks that Vince was involved in Sally's death and you didn't tell me." Her voice hardened, her body stiffening more with each word.

"What was I meant to say?" Liam widened his arms in a gesture of defense. "The guy you were going to marry is a terrorist and a murderer?"

"He's no different than you."

Her words cut him to the core. He could feel the blood draining from his face. "*What?* There's a massive difference between us. I haven't killed anyone."

"*Yet*. You said you were planning on hunting down the men responsible for Sally's death and murdering them. That includes Vince. And that, my friend, makes you no better than those men who killed your wife and whoever blew up the restaurant last night."

Liam shifted, her words piercing his soul. "But..."

"No buts. Thinking it is the same as if you had already done it. You passed the information to your brother. Let him and the authorities handle it." She stormed from the room, slamming the door behind her.

Liam stood there for a moment, then flung the door open and ran down the hall after her. He pushed open the bedroom door before she could close it. "Wait a second."

"What?" Her dark eyes glittered with rage and disappointment.

"There's a huge difference between them and me. They slaughtered those people for no reason. I was doing it for the sake of justice." He deliberately used the past tense. He'd promised Patrick he wouldn't go. He hadn't booked the flights or packed or anything. The feelings were still there, but so was the desire to drink. And he hadn't acted on that, either.

"No, Liam. You wanted revenge. Pure and simple. Justice comes from God and the law. You're neither."

"How do you know God won't use me, like He used Samson and David?" The argument sounded weak even to him.

"Don't try and justify it." Jacqui picked up the Bible from the bedside table. "Romans twelve says, '*Do not repay anyone evil for evil. Do not take revenge, my friends, but leave room for God's wrath, for it is written: "It is mine to avenge, I will repay," says the Lord.'*" She looked at him, her gaze going straight through him. "What you're planning is wrong. No make that *wrong* with a capital W."

Liam took a deep breath. "What Vince and his men did was wrong. Why are you madder at me than at him? I'm the one who lost here."

"Because you *know* it's wrong. You claim to be a Christian, and you say you rekindled your faith, but all along you were planning *this?* How do I know, more importantly how does God know you meant a word of it? Maybe it was a ruse to get me and keep me in your life."

Another spear pierced his soul, physically

knocking him a step backwards with the force of the blow. "It wasn't. I meant it. I love you. I want to honor God by what I do, but I also wanted to bring those responsible for Sally's death to justice."

Jacqui laid a gentle hand on his arm. "Liam, you have to let go and leave it to the police handle. If they don't, God will see the murderers pay for what they did. It's not up to you. Let it go."

"How?" The word was torn from him, another blow digging into the wall surrounding his heart.

"Pray."

"I have, but..."

"Stop with these buts." She pushed her hair back from her face, barely controlled irritation on her face. "God doesn't want to hear them any more than I do. He doesn't just want part of your life, Liam. He wants *all* of it. Isaiah chapter one says, *'When you spread out your hands in prayer, I will hide My eyes from you; even if you offer many prayers, I will not listen. Your hands are full of blood; wash and make yourselves clean. Take your evil deeds out of My sight.'*"

Liam's heart stopped and he dropped his gaze to the floor. His stomach roiled, his throat burned and his soul ached within him. "Oh."

"It's no good saying one thing when you're intent on doing another. God knows what you're thinking. And thinking it is as bad as doing it. Let God handle it."

Liam sank to his knees by the bed. How could he have gotten it so wrong? He was dimly aware of Jacqui kneeling beside him as he prayed.

Her voice joined his.

And then like the clouds of a thunderstorm passing, he was flooded with a sense of peace. The burden he carried for so long completely fell away.

Clare Revell

15

The doorbell rang, and Liam pushed up off his knees to answer it. He was stiffer than he realized. He opened the door to find Patrick and a uniformed officer standing there. "Hi."

"You all right, bro? We've been knocking for a while."

"Yeah, sorry. I wasn't expecting anyone this early."

Patrick raised an eyebrow. "It's gone ten AM. It's not early."

Ten? Where had the last few hours had gone? Last he knew, it was five something. "Sorry. Come in." He shut the door behind them. "Go through to the kitchen, and I'll get dressed."

He went back to the bedroom, knocking on the door. He smiled at Jacqui as she opened it, glad she was dressed.

"I found something of yours to wear." Jacqui held out her ruined dress. "This is beyond redemption."

He smiled, taking in the shirt and tracksuit trousers she'd put on. "That's fine."

"Who was at the door?"

"It's Patrick and the police."

"This doesn't look good, does it?"

He shook his head. "Apparently, we lost five hours. It's gone ten."

She squeezed his hand, sending an electrical

166

charge through him. He never wanted to take that for granted. "Time spent with God is not lost. Get dressed, and I'll go make them coffee."

He winked. "Good thing it's Saturday. Else we'd both be late for work."

"Oh yeah. Although then the alarm would have gone on my phone. It's set to go off at seven AM on a weekday."

Liam dressed and headed back to the kitchen. Jacqui sat at the table talking to the uniformed officer, telling him the events of the previous night as she remembered them. He crossed the room, picked up the spare mug of coffee, and turned to find Patrick standing behind him. "Hey, Pi."

"She said she spent the night here. And she's wearing your clothes."

"I had the couch. Not that either of us slept much. And that would be because her dress is ruined. Apparently being blown up and women's clothes don't go so well together."

"I can understand that."

Liam sipped the coffee. "How do you do this for a living?"

"Some days I wonder. Listen, once you've given your statement and the police leave, I need to talk to both you and Jacqui."

"Sounds ominous."

"It's important, Li. I wouldn't ask otherwise." Patrick lowered his voice. "One more thing? Leave out the incident in the gents for now. I know Jacqui knows, and I also asked her to keep quiet. If the cop asks, you got those bruises from the bomb blast. Let's face it; being blown across the car park probably gave you another one anyway."

Liam gave him a long hard look and then nodded. "It definitely didn't help any."

Patrick nodded. "Let's go sit down."

Liam sat at the table next to Jacqui and gave his statement. Going through it again was almost as bad as being there, just not so terrifying. Once that was done, he saw the officer out and then went back to the kitchen. He grinned at Patrick. "So Patrick, this is Jacqui. Jacqui, this reprobate is my big brother, Patrick. Otherwise known as Pi or Special Agent Three Point One Four."

Patrick grinned. "We met. Last night, remember? Fire, smoke, brimstone...well no brimstone, but you know what I mean."

Liam smacked Patrick on the back of the head. "No, I forgot. Getting blown up does that to a man, but at least I'm not old and grey like you."

Patrick laughed. "Less of the grey. It's about five hairs worth."

"So, what did you want to talk to me about?" Liam asked.

"How much do you both know about Vince Devlin?"

"Not much more than what you told me and we learnt last night over dinner." Liam winced. He'd forgotten for a moment how much his ribs hurt. "I told Jacqui everything I know and vice versa, which isn't much, but anyway...yeah...Mind filling in the gaps for us, bro?"

"Right, the Horatio Corporation owns the land the Endarra mission is built on. It bought the entire complex six months before the attack. They also own the mining rights to the surrounding area. We're pretty sure that whatever Devlin wants to rebuild there isn't an orphanage."

Liam pushed his empty cup away. "Can't you put someone on the inside?"

"We've tried doing that several times. Devlin's too good. He's also very good at keeping his nose clean." Patrick looked at Liam. "I tried contacting Manu. No one has seen or heard from him for three weeks."

"That's strange. He doesn't normally drop off the radar without saying something first." He pulled the phone from his pocket. "Let me try ring—"

"Li…wait." He slid a photo across the table. "Is this him?"

Liam recognized that smile and those eyes. Not to mention the shock of dyed blond hair which always looked strange against Manu's dark skin. "Yeah, that's him. Why do you ask?"

"He's dead." Patrick said.

Liam felt the blood drain from his face, and closed his eyes. He was aware of Jacqui gripping his hand tightly. He looked at his brother. "What about his wife and kids?"

"I'm sorry, bro." Patrick shook his head.

Jacqui wrapped her arms around him.

He hugged her back. *Oh, Lord, is that my fault somehow? I rang him on an unsecure line that last time. Am I responsible?*

"Before you go blaming yourself, don't. It looks as if Devlin is tidying up all the loose ends out there. Anyone who had anything to do with the original mission site is gradually vanishing or turning up dead."

Jacqui hugged Liam again. "You OK?"

"He's in God's hands, with his family. Manu was a believer. But it's still a loss. He was my friend." He looked up at Patrick. "So, what do we do now? Are you going to send someone out there? Get the African authorities to do something? It's not just foreign nationals he's killing now, it's their own people."

Patrick's expression became more serious. "It's not that simple."

He sighed. "No, it wouldn't be. It never is."

"I need you both to help me. I've been asked to ask you both—that's why we're doing this now and not in front of the cops."

"Oh?"

"We need to find out what's going on in Endarra. Like I said, we've tried and failed several times to get someone inside the offices. The easiest way by far, is to use someone Devlin wants, and get them into the Horatio Corporation and sent out there." Patrick looked at Jacqui.

"Me?" Jacqui caught her breath. "You want me to take the job?"

"*What?*" Liam asked, sitting bolt upright.

"Yes, Jacqui, we want you to take the job. Term finishes on Tuesday, and I understand from Liam that the school grounds will be finished then, too. At least enough for you to take a break for a week or so. That gives you the opportunity to take Devlin up on his offer and go out to see what's happening on site."

"Wait a minute," Liam interrupted. "Why send Jacqui? I told you what he did to her. Why not send one of your spooks?"

"I explained that. By now Devlin knows we're investigating the Horatio Corporation. He'll be expecting something. What he won't expect is for Jacqui to go in."

Jacqui shook her head. "There has to be another

way. He hurt me once. He'll do it again given half the chance."

Patrick looked at Jacqui. "There is no other way to do this. And you won't be going in alone. The thing is Vince wants you, and we want you to insist Liam goes, too."

"Me?"

"Li, you know the area. Most of the people you knew are gone, or dead. However, because you've been there, you can create a bond with the people, because of that familiarity. If there's something going on, they're more likely to talk to you than someone who doesn't understand their customs. Don't worry. You'll have back up—one of the catering staff is going to need to come back to England to tend to a sick relative and one of my people will replace them—"

"Then you don't need us. Can't he or she snoop around and—"

Patrick sighed. "Will you just be quiet and listen? Catering staff can't snoop around the entire site and the offices. Devlin will want to show off his operation to Jacqui. I'll send you in with a gun."

Liam shook his head. "I don't want one. I have all the ammunition and protection I need in God."

"You'll take the gun, Li. I don't want to lose you, too."

"And I told you, I'm not taking one. End of debate."

"Liam, you have no idea what you're getting into."

"Yes I do." Liam grimaced. "Is this where we get the 'Your country needs you' speech? In case you hadn't noticed, I'm a teacher, and Jacqui's a gardener." He broke off as she thumped him on the arm. "Sorry, my bad. Jacqui's a landscape architect. We're not spies."

"What's changed?" Patrick asked bluntly. "Two days ago, you were screaming out for the chance for revenge."

"God will do that. Isn't that what you told me months ago? Jacqui said the same thing this morning. It took a while to get through this thick head of mine."

"You mean God used a woman to get through to you when I couldn't."

"Something like that."

"I want each of you to pack a bag and go away for the weekend. A taxi will pick each of you up in an hour and take you to the station. From there you take the train to Bramley. A car will meet you there and drive you to a secret location for briefing and training in what you'll need to know."

Liam looked at Jacqui. "Up to you. I'm just the sidekick. The Dr. Watson to your Holmes, the Spock to your Kirk, the Patrick Starr to your SpongeBob, the Rudolph—"

"All right, OK, enough. I get it."

"So, what do you think, love? I know you don't want that creep anywhere near you, but I promise if he touches you at all, he'll regret it."

"I guess they wouldn't ask if they didn't really need us."

Her palm was warm and he looked down, slowly moving his thumb across the back of her hand. "It's ironic, isn't it? I've been asking God for months for this chance, and the minute I stop asking and hand it over to Him to deal with, He gives it to me on a plate. Bit like John the Baptist's head, only slightly less messy."

"So it's a yes?" Patrick asked.

"You don't actually want his head on a platter, do you?" Liam glanced at him.

"No. Thanks for the offer, bro, but no. We'd rather lock him up and throw away the key."

"We'll talk it over, pray it through, and get back to you."

"I can't give you any longer. The taxi's coming for you in less than an hour."

Liam took a deep breath. *Lord, show me what to do. I can't let her go alone and as much as I want to go out there...* He paused, a sudden sense that he was doing the right thing flooding him. *All right, but You have to come, too. I'm not doing this without You by my side.*

"Maybe you get to be Samson after all." Jacqui squeezed his hand.

"Only if you be Delilah." Liam nodded. "However, I don't want their fates. We get to live happily ever after. Don't want from here to Endarra turning into from here to eternity."

"We'll make Samson and Delilah your code names." Patrick handed Jacqui the phone. "Make the call and put it on speaker phone. But don't let him arrange the flights. We'll do that."

Jacqui nodded. Her hands shaking, she dialed Vince's number.

"Devlin."

"Hi, Vince. It's Jacqui."

"Jacqui, baby, how are you? I was worried after the fire last night. Are you all right?"

"I'm fine. Listen, Liam and I were talking, and we could both do with a break."

"I assume that means you decided to take the job. That's great, hon. The old team together again."

"No. Actually it means that Liam and I will both

come out, and you can show us what needs doing. Then I'll make an informed decision."

"I'll book you a flight. It'll be wonderful to spend some time alone with you."

"Liam and I will book our own flights." She looked at Patrick as he scrawled a note and handed it to her. She read it and nodded her understanding. "We're going to a couple of places first and figured we'd add Endarra on to the end of our trip."

"And what if I don't want Liam to come?"

"Then I don't come. Liam is part of my life, and he's agreed to fit this into our holiday. So it's both of us, or neither."

Vince's voice tightened. "Fine. When will you arrive?"

"I'll let you know when we've booked the flight. Speak to you then." She hung up and looked at Liam. "All right. Let's go learn how to be spies."

Liam reached over and kissed her. "Only so long as I can be the spy that loved you."

She shook her head. "Your jokes get worse." She looked at Patrick. "Can you drop me off so I can pack?"

Patrick nodded. "Of course."

Jacqui stood and kissed Liam. "I'll see you in an hour."

16

Jacqui and Liam exited the plane and headed into immigration and customs hand in hand. Jacqui felt woefully unprepared despite the training she'd been given. Vince had arranged to pick them up, and she made the most of the last few moments alone with Liam. She handed over her passport and tried not to squirm as the officer fixed his steel gaze on her.

"What is the reason for your visit?"

"Vacation." She took a deep breath, hoping she hadn't changed too much from her photograph as he compared the two

"Where are you staying?"

"The *Matumaini* mission."

"Are you with the Horatio Corporation?"

She nodded.

The officer handed back her papers and waved her though with no more checks. *Strange…let's just hope Liam finds it as easy.*

Jacqui stood to one side.

Liam collected his bags and was escorted away from the queue and into a side room.

Now what? How did she get through and Liam didn't? Was he the random fifth passenger they did extra checks on, or was it something more sinister? Perhaps Vince's hand was in all this. He didn't want Liam here; maybe he'd had a red flag put against his name to deny him entry to the country. She knew how deep Vince's fingers went and just what he was capable of.

She sat down on a chair and closed her eyes, praying hard. Right now there was only One person who could get Liam out of this mess and fortunately she had His number. *Lord, please intervene here. I need him. Don't let them refuse him entry. He didn't pack the gun, despite Patrick giving him one, he left it at home.* Jacqui was still praying ten minutes later when someone sat in the chair beside her.

"Wake up," said a very familiar Irish lilt. "We have places to go and people to see."

"Liam...are you all right? I was so worried."

"You're not the only one. My name must have flagged something. They unpacked my bags and asked a dozen questions and then some. But once I mentioned I was here with the Horatio Corporation, they backed right off."

"I guess Vince has his uses after all. Though it was probably Vince who flagged your name in the first place."

"Yeah, more than likely. He probably wanted to be sure I was unarmed. So, are we going to go face our friend Vince?" He pulled out his mobile phone. "At least there's coverage here." He tapped quickly and sent a short concise text message. He hadn't even put the phone away before, he got a reply. He deleted the message then leaned over to whisper in Jacqui's ear, pretending to kiss her on the neck.

"All righty. He knows we're here and wants me to report in again in six hours. Assuming we're there, then. And the new cook apparently goes by the name Rhubarb, or Dennis if you want his real name. If we want to get a message to Patrick, other than by normal means, we ask for chicken and sage dumplings when we go to eat."

"All very cloak and dagger, isn't it?" Jacqui murmured back, tracing a kiss against his jaw.

"I can see it now. 'What did you do during the summer holiday, Sir?' 'I worked for MI5 as a spy. My name is Page, Liam Page, Agent Double Oh Eight Point Five, with a license to panic. You think they'd believe me if I told them?" He continued whispering.

"Nope. However, when we get home you could write a book entitled *My Life as a Spy by The Head of the English Department*. It could be a required exam reading in years to come." Her voice was as soft as the kiss she landed on his mouth.

"Yeah, right. All joking aside, this may get dangerous. However, God is on our side." He sobered and gripped her hand. "All right. Better go before he wonders where we are."

Jacqui stood with him and added her bags to his trolley. She let Liam lead her through the double doors to where Vince stood. The hair on the back of her neck rose as she got closer to him.

Vince shook Liam's hand, dropping it quickly, and then pulled Jacqui into a hug. "How was your flight? There was no need for you to fly commercial. I could have sent the company jet for you and saved you both the air fare."

Jacqui twisted free, her skin crawling. "The flight was fine, thank you. Like I explained on the phone, we're on holiday so it's not a problem us doing it. Besides, the airline food is an adventure in itself." *And a commercial flight means there's an official record of us entering the country.*

"I've got transport waiting outside. It'll take us to

the compound."

Grateful for Liam's firm grip on her hand, Jacqui followed Vince out of the air-conditioned airport into the bright sunlight. The heat hit her like a blast furnace, taking her breath away. She pulled her shades over her eyes and tugged her hat down further.

Vince's driver slung the bags into the boot before opening the door to for Jacqui and Liam. Vince got in the other side of Jacqui.

The Land Rover bounced over the potholes and uneven surfaces.

Jacqui slid her hand into Liam's. He was pale, and she wasn't sure if he was car sick or just overwhelmed with memories. "Are you all right?"

He shook his head. "No. I feel sick." He grabbed the door as the truck leaped over a hump in the road.

"Stop the truck," Jacqui said as the last of the color drained from Liam's face. The truck squealed to a halt in a spray of gravel.

Liam flung the door open and staggered out and over to the side of the road.

Jacqui gave him a few minutes, then slid out of the truck and went over to him. "Liam?"

He wiped his hand over his mouth and straightened up. "I'm all right."

"Are you sure?"

He took a deep breath. "Yeah."

Jacqui handed him a bottle of water. "Drink some of this. It'll help."

"Thanks, love."

She watched him as he took a long drink of the water. *Is he going to manage this? Is the bravado for my benefit or simply a way to hide his true feelings from everyone?* "Is it much further?"

"I'm not sure. I only drove it the once. They flew us out."

"We need to go." Vince yelled from the car, his glare as dark as Liam was pale. "Or we won't make it by dark."

"We're coming." Taking hold of Liam's hand, she led him back over to the Rover.

****

It was dark when they arrived. Two overhead lights illuminated the sign over the huge gates and several more lit the compound behind it. Barbed wire fences disappeared into the night. Armed guards stood in the tower by the gate.

"Are you keeping something in or something out?" Jacqui looked at Vince.

"Out," came the stern reply. "The local wildlife isn't tame by any stretch of the imagination. You'll find the accommodation here basic to say the least. The showers and latrines are unisex, mainly as there are no women here. Except you that is. There is a dining hut and dorms. But I have set aside a room for each of you in what used to be staff quarters here. Most of the complex is in ruins. We are still working on clearing it."

The truck stopped and Vince leapt out. "I'll show you to your rooms. Someone will fetch you when it's time to eat."

Jacqui could see Liam's distaste at the thought of dinner. She turned back to Vince. "Actually, I might give dinner a miss tonight. It's been a long day and I'm shattered. I might just hit the hay and sleep until morning."

"Sounds like an excellent plan." Liam was quick to agree.

Vince scowled, but nodded. "Very well." Vince beckoned one of the men over. "This is Simeon. He will show you to your rooms. His English is basic but adequate. He says what he needs in as few words as possible."

Liam gripped her hand tightly as Jacqui followed Simeon across the compound.

Vince was apparently offended, as he delegated the task rather than taking them himself. *Good job Simeon is wearing a white shirt else we wouldn't see him.* The man was armed, even inside the fence. Surely they were safe in here.

Simeon pointed out the buildings as they passed, explaining their uses. "Meal hut. A gong sounds and tells you when it's time to eat. New cook, but he very good. Shower hut. Hot water only last three minutes per person. Wash quickly."

Liam frowned. "Only three minutes of hot water? I might have to go and find the river and bathe there."

Simeon's head flew back and forth sharply. "You stay away from river. Many crocodiles—eat you for lunch."

Liam sighed and looked at Jacqui. "I guess that rules out pooh sticks then."

She pulled a sad face. "I guess so. We'll have to find something else to do instead."

"Latrines…" Simeon ignored them and pointed to another building. He looked at Jacqui. "I arrange one with sign on for just you, memsahib."

"No, please don't. Its fine just the way it is."

Simeon nodded as his feet clattered up wooden steps and down the verandah.

Laughter echoed from one of the other rooms.

"Keep the screens closed, keep mosquito out. You have, uh, how you say, quynyne?"

"Quinine?" Liam asked.

"Yes, little white tablet?" He smiled as they both nodded. "Good. You need them. Take often." He pushed open two doors. "This one your room, memsahib. Try not leaving your room alone after dark. Not safe." He shot her another beaming smile and left.

Jacqui looked at Liam, to find a matching grin on his face. "What?"

"Think someone likes you."

"Yeah, you." She eased her shoulders. "I could do with a shower."

Liam nodded. "I'll come with you. I don't really want you wandering around alone in the dark. Though honestly, with those lights and armed guards, it probably is safe—but there's more than the wildlife to worry about. I'll protect you from the vipers."

"That's very gallant of you. You sure it has nothing to do with the showers being unisex?"

"Nothing at all." Liam's laugh echoed on the wooden verandah. "I just don't want to have to mount a search party to come find you when you get lost."

"When? Don't you mean *if* I get lost?"

"I never say anything I don't mean, *memsahib*." He imitated the young man's admiring tone.

"Don't you start. I'll just unpack my towel and stuff."

Liam put a hand on her arm and frowned.

"What is it?"

"Humor me. Swap rooms, but don't tell anyone. If I remember rightly, there's door leading to a back verandah. We can go in and out unseen through them."

"This is getting stranger by the second."

"Yes, but it might keep us safe." He went through his door.

Jacqui went into her room, jumping as she realized Liam was already there. "How did you…?" She broke off as he pointed silently to the door between the two rooms. "Ah…"

"This is even better than going out the back and back in again. If you leave this one unlocked I can be in here in a flash."

She smiled and went through the door into the other room. A quick glance to her left showed another door in that wall too. She locked it and looked at it. "It'll be fairly easy to break it down. It looks pretty flimsy. I'll move something heavy in front of it as well. Maybe the chest of drawers."

"I'll do it now for you."

"That's very gallant of you."

He pretended to tip his hat. "Oh, to be sure, to be sure, Miss Jacqui."

Glancing around the rest of the room, she took in the simple furniture. As well as the set of drawers which Liam was manhandling across the room, there was a bed, and nightstand—simple but livable for the few days she would be here. A mosquito net hung over the bed and despite the darkness and open window, the heat was stifling. She put her bag on the floor by the bed and pulled out a towel, wash stuff and change of clothes. Three minutes was ample time, no matter what Liam said.

The shower block was busy and Jacqui got more than one appreciative stare as she entered. She ignored the scantily clad men—who made no effort to cover themselves—and headed to the bank of cubicles. She was relieved to find each stall had a lockable door and enough room to dry and dress. Turning on the water, she stood under it, fully dressed, letting the water soak in to her clothes as it heated up.

Stripping off, Jacqui made the most of her three minutes of hot water. A smile crossed her face as she heard Liam singing over the sound of the water. Just as the hot water ran out, she finished rinsing her hair. She hopped out of the shower letting the cold water rinse her clothes. She dried and dressed quickly and then wrung out her things, before wrapping them in her towel. Opening the door she found Liam standing in front of it. "That's better. Feel half human again now."

He smiled at her. "Me too. I might feel fully human after a few hours' sleep." He yawned. "I'm about ready to sleep now." He slid his hand into hers, and they headed out into the night. The sounds of the jungle filled the air as they walked. "I'll knock for you about eight. That way we can start the day in prayer."

"That sounds good to me." Jacqui paused outside the door to her room and kissed his cheek. "Good night."

"Don't I get a proper kiss?" Liam wrapped his arms around her and lowered his voice. "We're being watched. Better stick to going in the proper doors and using the connecting one to switch. And it doesn't hurt to emphasize the fact that you're my girl, Jacqui Dorne. Mine, and no one else's."

"Any excuse," she murmured as he kissed her. She closed her eyes, letting the scent of shampoo and shower gel fill her senses. His hands ran over her arms, sending shivers of pleasure through her, pulling her close as he deepened the kiss. Her head spun with the sensations filling her.

As he broke the kiss, she stood still, content to be in his arms a little longer. "There's no one else's girl I'd rather be. Just like you're my man."

"Now that sounds good. Are you going to stand by me, then?"

"To the end. Are you all right? Being here again, I mean?"

"Yeah," he replied after a while, his voice taut with grief and emotion. "I'm not denying it's hard, much harder than I thought it would be. Sally and I...we'd sit on the verandah at night, listening to the jungle sounds, a little like we are now. She'd sing hymns and I'd read."

"I can sing if you want."

"No, it's fine, thank you. I've heard you sing." He kissed her gently. "Goodnight."

"Goodnight." She went into the room, knowing he'd stand there until she locked the door, then she headed into the other room. She smiled as he came in and locked the door behind him. "Goodnight. Again."

Liam shook his head as he went into the other room. "See you at seven."

"Seven? I thought you said eight."

"I did. But if I'm knocking on your door at eight, then we need to be up and dressed first. Especially as I have to go through your room in order to get out."

"Ah, I hadn't thought of that. It's confusing, all this room switching."

"Confusing, aye, But necessary." The door clicked shut behind him.

Jacqui moved to the windows, pulling the shutters closed. Dusting off her hands, she crossed to the bed and pulled her Bible from her bag before lying on the bed.

The huge ceiling fan provided some relief from the heat, but not much. The netting made her enclosed bed hotter than an oven. It was, however, better than being bitten by a million mosquitoes. Checking the Bible notes, she turned to the evening passage in Zephaniah chapter three verse seventeen. *The LORD your God is with you, He is mighty to save. He will take great delight in you, He will quiet you with His love, He will rejoice over you with singing.*

17

Liam jerked awake, his heart pounding as he sat bolt upright. What had woken him? He glanced at his watch and pressed the back light button. Surprisingly it was only eleven thirty, although it felt so much later. The sound came again. Footsteps on the wooden verandah stopped outside his door. He pushed back the thin sheet and stood. He crept silently to the door just as the handle moved. The door shook a little and he was very grateful it was locked.

"Jacqui, are you awake?"

Vince? What did he want?

"Jacqui?"

Liam prayed that she was sleeping soundly in the next room and if not she had the sense not to answer if she heard him. The door shook again, then the footsteps moved away. Liam sat by the door, praying for protection for the both of them while they were here for half an hour before going back to bed.

What seemed like only moments later, his alarm went off loudly and insistently. He thumped it and opened his eyes. Sunshine glinted around the shutters. He lay there for a while. Had he dreamt the events of the previous night? Either way he wasn't going to tell Jacqui. She didn't need to know. It would only worry her, and there was enough to worry about as it was. But his spur of the moment decision to swap rooms, was already paying dividends.

Stretching he stood and pulled out a change of clothes. Deciding on the usual trousers rather than shorts, he dressed. He'd packed them on Patrick's say so, but hadn't worn shorts since he was shot, choosing to hide the scars that so disfigured him. For one thing, if Terry hadn't already worked out whom he was, bullet scarred legs would tell the entire world. And for another—he wasn't ready to reveal those scars to Jacqui, just yet.

Stretching again, Liam pushed his hands though his hair and then reapplied the deodorant. It was far too hot here, much hotter than he remembered. He buttoned his shirt as he wandered over to the window and flung the shutters open wide.

His whole body went numb with shock. Hair stood up on the back of his neck. Burned out buildings lined the side of the compound immediately opposite, the remains of the school house, offices, refectory. The steps Sally had been standing on led up to a shell. The burned chapel stood to the right, and the destroyed play area to the left.

For the first few months after Sally died, Liam had seen the attack play out in his dreams night after night. He heard the screams, gunshots and crackling of the hungry flames which ate everything around him. Since Jacqui came into his life, the dreams had diminished, but this brought the images crashing back with a vengeance.

He staggered backwards, choking and gasping for breath. He sagged down onto the bed, his hands over his face. He could see it in front of him—the gunmen appearing and firing, the bullets spinning Sally around, before ripping into him. His jaw, shoulder and knee hurt like they hadn't in a while. Fire exploded around them as he crawled to where his wife laid bleeding and dying. The smoke was raw and bitter in the back of his throat. Tears burned his eyes as he struggled to breathe.

He didn't know how long he sat there before the connecting door opened and closed and Jacqui pulled him into her arms. He was aware of her speaking, but it took a few seconds to realize she was praying. When she finished, he looked up at her, his cheeks wet and his eyes sore. He hadn't even realized he was crying. It was something he never allowed himself to do. He hadn't cried for Sally since she died.

Jacqui pushed a hand through his hair and down his face. "Better?"

"Yeah. Sorry, it's just so hard being here."

"It's all right. I understand."

Liam rubbed his hand over his eyes and leaned into her touch. He relished the contact, needing the love she offered in the place of so much death and destruction. "Good job, there's a connecting door. I almost locked it last night."

"I had a plan if you had. I'd have convinced Simeon I'd locked myself out and got him to let me back in. No doubt he has keys for everything."

Liam nodded. He needed to tell her to put a chair under her door, just in case Vince decided to come calling again.

Jacqui kissed him gently, not moving her hand, and he returned the kiss, wrapping his arms tightly around her. For a few minutes nothing mattered except being there with her. Then she pulled back slowly and looked at him. "Want to tell me about it?"

He took a deep breath and pointed to the window. "That central ruin was the school house. Sally was standing on the steps. She'd just finished teaching the kids a new song—the wise man built his house upon the rock. The gunmen came from all sides, cutting off any chance we had of getting out, firing simultaneously. For a moment, it was like it was happening all over again. I could see it, and feel the bullets tearing into me..."

"Show me?" Jacqui asked.

Liam undid his shirt and pushed it back off his shoulder showing Jacqui the scar running across his shoulder. If she was going to reject him it would be now, once she saw his scars and how deep they ran.

She'd seen this one before.

He didn't look at her, keeping his gaze on the wall behind her, and wondered if she were abhorred by what she saw.

"I know it's pretty horrible." He tried to pull his shirt back up, but she stilled his hands with a tender touch.

"Shhh…"

Liam closed his eyes as Jacqui traced the scar with gentle fingertips. She lowered her head and soft lips touched the scars. Deep radiating heat blossomed from where she touched him, circling downwards and tightening across his stomach. He swallowed hard. This wasn't what he'd expected. He hated them so much, he…

When she didn't speak, he took a deep breath, needing to break the all-consuming silence that had fallen, broken only by their breathing. "The docs were amazed I got any movement back in my shoulder, at all. I'll never throw the shot put or javelin again, but I teach English, not sport. I got the same reaction from them over my other injuries. I guess God just wasn't ready for me and thought I'd be more useful here."

Jacqui cupped his face, turning it towards her. Her eyes shone with unshed tears, matching the ones he knew were burning in his own eyes. "Show me."

Was he imagining the depth of love in her voice as she repeated her simple request? Did she realize just what she was doing to him? She was peeling him back, layer by layer, exposing every scar and emotion he'd kept buried the last couple of years. He held her gaze for a moment, and then nodded. He pushed up his trousers to just above his knee. Again her gentle touch traced the outline of the long jagged scar which ran across the knee.

"It aches when it rains, but I can walk and run and bend to lift things."

He took her fingers and ran them along the scar under his beard. "There is one here as well. That one could have done more damage."

Jacqui traced along the scar, her eyes following it. "You missed one."

"I did?" Confusion filled him. "I don't think so. Three bullets—shoulder, knee and jaw."

She placed her hand gently on his chest, and his heart started pounding so fast he thought it would jump from his chest. Fire leapt through his skin, igniting the embers with in him. No one had touched him since Sally...he looked up, aware she was speaking.

"...here, too. Perhaps the worst scar. Part of you died when Sally and the others did."

He nodded, his hand resting on hers. "But being here with you...I think God put you in my life at the right time. To show me that there is life, and love, in the midst of sorrow."

"And beauty, too."

Liam shook his head, reluctantly breaking the contact and moving her hand. If she stayed touching his bare chest, the temptation he was feeling might prove too much. "My scars aren't pretty." He started to do up his shirt. "None of them are."

"They're part of you, so they have their own beauty."

"They're not. I'm not…"

Her hands covered his for a moment, and stilled them. Her fingers retraced the scar on his shoulder, her light touch searing his skin. "They prove you'd do anything to protect someone you love, and that is the true mark of beauty."

Liam grabbed her fingers and kissed them. "I wish this were over. Right now, I'd give anything for us to be a hundred miles from here..."

"I know, but you're not alone. I'm right here with you."

"I need you." He wrapped his arms around her, pulling her close. "Let's do this and go home."

"Who'd think a teacher and a landscape architect would ever be used as spies?"

"Not me. In fact, if you told me when I first tipped flowers over your laptop that we'd end up here, I'd have laughed."

"Not as much as Eve and Holly did. You wouldn't believe the number of times I heard the 'say it with flowers' joke."

"One of Niamh's boyfriends dug out the entire front garden overnight and planted flowers all over it. When she opened her curtains in the morning 'Marry me Niamh' was there in blooms."

"Wonderful. I assume she said yes."

"And then Jared had to put the lawn back to rights again. He decided it was worth it. Only he wasn't finished. Two weeks later Niamh opened the curtains to find 'She said yes' again written in flowers."

Jacqui shook her head, moving her hands so he could do up his shirt. "Funny."

He took a deep breath as the gong sounded. "I'm not hungry, but we should probably try to eat. Especially as we skipped dinner last night, on top of not eating much yesterday."

"Yeah, we'll need all the strength we can get today. How about we go eat and then come back and pray for guidance and protection?"

"Now that sounds like a plan."

"And we can check out the new cook at the same time. If he's Rhubarb, I want to know who Custard is."

"I don't know and I'm not going to let you 'check him out'. I might get jealous and turn into a hulking green monster."

Jacqui snorted. "Actually, you could be sky blue pink with yellow dots, and I'll still like you."

Liam kissed her fingers. "Like you back. And your front and your side…"

"Get on with you," she laughed. "Let's go before it all gets eaten."

****

An hour later, Liam led Jacqui over to where Vince stood waiting under the shade of the tree. Liam couldn't help but notice how the scowl on Vince's face darkened as he and Jacqui walked over, fingers linked. Hopefully, Vince would get the message loud and clear that Jacqui was his girl now and not to be touched. His smile widened at the thought.

Vince spoke first. "Good morning. We'll start with the tour and then I'll tell you what I have envisioned for here."

"All right."

As they walked across the compound, Vince described his plans for the place. Liam listened in amazement. What happened to Jacqui having free reign in the design of this place? Vince didn't want her designs or ideas at all. He had this planned down to the tiniest detail. What was Vince really up to here?

Liam mentally listed everything from gunrunning to drugs to diamond smuggling. He tightened his grip on Jacqui and froze. They were standing in the central compound in front of the burned out buildings.

"The main massacre was here. A young blonde woman was teaching a class of children. She and her class died right where we're standing."

"Vince, is all this detail necessary?" Jacqui asked. "We get that they died here. I thought you wanted me to redesign it, but you seem to have sorted that."

"Then walk with me, and tell me what you would do here."

"All right." She didn't let go of Liam.

Vince held out a hand to her. "Alone."

"We'll both come." Liam tightened his grip on her hand.

"Alone," Vince insisted.

"I don't think so." Liam looked at Vince. "Like she said, she wants my opinion on this. Although it sounds to me like you have everything pretty well organized."

"Actually, yes, I have."

"Then you really don't need us. I'm sure you can find another pretty face to rubber stamp this for you."

Liam stood his ground.

Vince moved over to him and lowered his voice. "If I didn't know any better, I'd say you were trying to stop her from being alone with me. Don't you trust her?"

"Stop talking about her as if she isn't here." Liam almost bubbled over with anger. What kind of man was this bloke? "I trust Jacqui with my life. So you need to ask her if she wants to be alone with you." *It's you I don't trust.*

"Jacqui do you want to walk with me for half an hour?" Vince dismissed Liam with a look. "I'm sure you can find something to do."

Liam looked at Jacqui. That *would* give him chance to look around Vince's office. As much as he didn't want Jacqui alone with him, he'd never get a better chance than now. He held her gaze for a moment then turned back to Vince and nodded slowly. "Half an hour is all you get, Vince."

Jacqui pulled Liam a few steps away, and then hugged him. "Be careful," she whispered in his ear. "I'll distract him as long as I can."

"You be careful, too. I love you." He wrapped his arms firmly around her, pulling her as close against him as he could. His lips traced a path of kisses from the base of her neck slowly up to her ear. He caught her earlobe, smiling against her cheek as she shivered, before pressing his lips firmly against hers. Her lips parted and he deepened the kiss, pouring every ounce of love and emotion into the kiss as he could. He could taste the coffee she'd drunk and her perfume filled his senses.

Jacqui finally broke the kiss and squeezed his hand. "What will you do?"

"I'll go lie on the bed and read for a bit." He hoped she'd catch on and play along.

"OK…will you be OK? You were awfully sick last night." She caught on.

Liam loosened her hand. "Go on—you fuss too much. I'm fine, love. Being sick yesterday would have been down to the heat and a long flight. Nothing more."

"Sure?"

"Yes, I'll see you at lunch." He pulled her into his arms and kissed her, her soft lips under his leaving him in no doubt as to how she felt about him. "I love you."

"I love you, too."

Liam kissed her again, and reluctantly let go and watched as Vince tried to take her hand.

Lord, go with her and keep her safe. While he's distracted I'll go and find the office and see what I can discover about Vince's true interest in this place. Go before me.

Jacqui tore her hand away from Vince's and shoved her hand into her pocket.

Liam glanced back across the compound and moved to the spot where Sally had died, saying a final goodbye. Then he took a deep breath and headed across the compound as nonchalantly as he could. He nodded to Simeon standing guard duty by the main gate. "There are a lot of security personnel here."

Simeon nodded. "There are a lot of wild animals."

"So you said last night, but I haven't heard anything but birds, never mind seen anything. And surely they wouldn't come inside the fence anyway."

"Sahib Devlin…he likes protection."

"He said the threat of attack was over."

"Sahib Devlin want memsahib kept safe. She will be *mke* soon."

Liam looked up sharply, hoping he'd heard incorrectly. *Mke* was wife. "*Mkewe*?" *His wife?*

Simeon nodded, lowering his voice. "He will take her as *mkewe*. He very grateful to you for bringing her here."

Liam's stomach turned. "When is this marriage happening?"

Simeon grinned, white teeth sparkling against the dark skin. "Tomorrow at sunset."

"I see. Well I'm glad I could help. I'm sure he'll be very happy." Liam moved away. *Lord, the time scale for this just upped a notch. Don't let him do anything to her. Let me find what I need so we can get out of here by tonight.* He had to warn Jacqui without Vince finding out.

He had to get into the office and go through the files. Then he needed to send a coded message to Patrick via the cook. That he could do over lunch.

Liam paused by the fence, gazing out through the wire. He'd forgotten how pretty it was here. His eyes traced the fence to the gates and the road beyond. If he could find a plausible reason to borrow a truck tonight, then perhaps he and Jacqui could leave, getting enough of a head start before Vince set the hounds after them.

Of course they could very well end up getting shot as they tried to leave. But that he'd place securely in God's hands. No amount of worrying would solve the problem.

Liam moved behind the ruins to where the new offices had been built. A barrel stood outside, incongruously filled with flowers. A lizard sat on the steps sunning itself, and a bird stood on the tin roof chirping as loudly as it could.

Vince's door stood open and, checking the coast was clear, Liam slid inside, shutting the door quietly behind him.

The office was tidy and nothing out of place. Liam moved to the desk and tried the drawers. Each one was locked. A folder lay open on the top, and Liam scanned the papers quickly. Nothing there. His attention was caught by two gold framed photographs. One showed Vince and Jacqui smiling at the camera, his arm around her waist. The other had Vince, Jacqui and an older couple.

He slid his fingers under the desk and found the key stuck to the underside. That was as reliable as keeping the spare door key under a flower pot, and a woman keeping all her valuables in the knicker drawer. Sally always had, and he knew his sister did too. Of course if the women knew that every man knew this, they'd find a different hiding place. He freed the key from the blu-tac holding it in place and unlocked the drawers. The first contained pens and pencils and a few odds and ends. The second contained files. His fingers roamed the folders, not sure what he was looking for. Then he paused, his heart growing cold. *Liam Page—why would he have a file on me?*

Liam pulled it out and read.

Vince knew who he was.

There were photos of him and Sally, some taken here.

"Oh Lord God, protect us," he whispered. He put the file back and pulled out another labeled Manu.

Vince *was* cleaning up the loose ends, just like Patrick said, he realized in horror as he read, but why?

What was so important that people like Sally and Manu had to die?

He slid Manu's file away and another caught his eye—Liberaté. He opened it, his eyes widening. So that was it. Laying the file on the table, he took the pen camera Patrick had given him and ran it over the papers. For the first time he regretted leaving the gun at home.

Just as he reached the last sheet, footsteps echoed outside.

Liam shoved the file back in the drawer and took a sheet of paper from the notepad, scribbling on it quickly.

The door rattled and Liam dived under the desk, shoving the pen back into his pocket. He pulled in tight as Vince's voice filled it. "And this is my office."

"Cozy." Jacqui sounded bored. Her light steps covered the room and he heard the photo frames moving. "Vince—you kept the one of us?"

"Of course I did. And the one of us with my parents. They loved you like a daughter. Why don't you sit at the desk and get a feel for it?"

"All right." Her tone indicated she was unsure, but the chair scraped back a little and creaked, before her perfume wafted over him.

Liam froze, his breathing echoing in the tiny space. Something kicked him, and he bit his tongue in an effort not to cry out. He glanced up, his gaze meeting Jacqui's. Then she looked up. "Nice desk. Although it's a little big and ornate for here, don't you think?"

"Maybe we put it in your office...or we can get you something similar."

"That's a little presumptuous, Vince. I haven't said yes yet."

"You will." His voice was nearer now. "Shall we move on?"

"All right." Jacqui's foot brushed up Liam's arm for a moment as she stood.

He caught her shoe, shoving the paper inside it, praying she'd either think nothing of it, or she'd only move it when she was alone.

"It's almost time for lunch anyway. And I should go and check on Liam. He said half an hour, and it's been more than that. I imagine he fell asleep." Her foot touched Liam's arm again then she moved back around the desk.

"Leave him to sleep. I can get the cook to save him some lunch."

"Oh…all right. If you're sure it's no trouble."

"Yes, I'm sure. It will be my pleasure." Vince's voice retreated across the room. "Then I have something special planned."

"What's that?"

"You'll see."

The footsteps left the room and echoed down the wooden boards outside. The pounding of his heart gradually slowed, and he wiped his damp palms on his trousers. After a moment or two longer, he slid out and headed to the door. He walked onto the verandah as nonchalantly as he could manage.

"What are you doing in there?" Terry's voice made him jump.

"I was looking for Jacqui. She was with Vince, and I thought he might know where she is."

"He's not here."

"I can see that. I'll go and see if she's at lunch."

"You do that. And stay away from the offices."

Liam headed down the steps and across to the

ruins, aware that Terry was right behind him. Halfway across the quad, a hand gripped his arm, spinning him around. "Simeon has already given me the good news about the wedding. Is this a best man to ex-boyfriend friendly warning chat? Afraid I might object and stop it going ahead?"

Terry looked at him, his eyes glittering. "You were here."

Liam nodded. There was no point denying it—especially as he now remembered where he had seen Terry before. "Yes, I was. So were you. I remember you, now."

"Do you now? And what else do you remember?"

"I thought I recognized you in the restaurant, but I've only just placed you. You led the assault on this place. You shouted the orders. You killed my wife."

"You're a smart man, even if you did survive. It's just a shame you left the restaurant when you did."

Liam stiffened. "I'm sorry?"

"If that man hadn't interfered, you'd be dead. It's like you have nine lives or something."

"I don't understand…"

"Vince knows who you are. He doesn't want you messing up his plans. He's dealing with the woman. Once she marries him tomorrow night, then she'll keep quiet. She won't be given a choice. And I get the pleasure of dealing with you and completing our unfinished business."

"I thought Vince was—" Blinding pain filled every part of Liam's body as something hard connected with the base of his skull. He dropped to his knees, gasping in pain. He blinked, trying to clear the double vision.

He had to find Jacqui. She wasn't safe here. *Lord, please...*

Another blow sent him to the ground, cutting off conscious thought, and he knew no more.

18

Jacqui ate her lunch and tried to ignore the fact that Vince sat too close, intruding on her personal space.

What was Liam doing hiding under Vince's desk? He must have been looking for something when they walked in. Hopefully, she'd get a chance to talk to him before long.

Terry came in and spoke quietly to Vince, handing him two pieces of paper.

She didn't catch what he said, but judging from the dark frown that settled on Vince's face, it wasn't good news. He glared at the paper so hard Jacqui wouldn't have been surprised to see flames leaping from it.

"Something wrong?" she asked.

Vince looked up. "Just business. And this one is for you. Liam sends his apologies. He wanted to go shopping, so one of the men drove him to the local market. He said to tell you he'd see you at dinner." He handed her the note, not bothering to apologize for having read it first.

Jacqui glanced at the paper. It wasn't Liam's writing, but probably one of the guards on the gate. "Oh, all right." Perhaps that's what he was trying to tell her earlier. But somehow she doubted it. Things were starting to add up, and she didn't like where it was headed at all. "I'm going to get dessert. Be right back." She pushed her chair back and stood. She really didn't want to be alone with Vince, but she no longer had a choice did she? Vince had seen to that.

What was that code phrase again? Why didn't I pay proper attention to all this? Think girl. Liam mentioned it at the airport. It was something to do with chicken and dumplings. God, please help me remember…

She stood in line and picked up one of the pieces of fruit. She turned it over in her hands, inspecting it.

The cook smiled at her. "It's a marula. A little like an orange, but it has a stone in the middle. You'll like it."

"Thank you. And thank you for lunch, it was wonderful. I was wondering if chicken and dumplings were on the menu for tonight."

"What kind of dumplings did you want?"

"Ummm…" *What kind were they?* Panic filled her, her mind going totally blank.

A hand touched her shoulder, sliding down her arm and covering her hand. "Are you chatting up my new cook?"

"I complimented him on his cooking," she said looking at Vince. "And I also asked if Liam had been in for lunch before he so thoughtlessly abandoned me for the rest of the day." She turned her gaze back to the cook. "I came to breakfast with him. Bit taller than Vince, he's got brown hair, beard, very pale as we haven't been here long."

"I remember him. I haven't seen him yet this meal, memsahib. But if I do, I'll be sure to tell him you're looking for him," the cook replied.

"Thank you." She prayed he'd got the message and would pass it on, even if she couldn't remember what flavor dumplings she should have asked for.

Vince smiled at her, his touch on her hand raising the hair on the back of her neck. "How about we take a Rover and go out and see the lions just north of here?"

"Lions?" *How appropriate—he looks like one closing in for the kill himself.*

"Pride Rock is only an hour from here. We could be there and back before dark. You could take some photos and show Liam what he missed out on."

"Yeah, sounds good. I'll go back and get my camera."

Vince kissed her hand, his lingering touch making her want another shower. "Don't be long. I'm missing you already."

Trying not to shiver, Jacqui turned. She'd only taken two steps when she heard him right behind her.

"Actually, I'll come with you. It'll be quicker. The sooner we leave here, the longer we'll have there."

****

Reaching the doors to the rooms, Jacqui stopped outside the one she should be in. "Stay here. Don't want to give everyone the wrong impression by inviting you into my room. Give me ten minutes or so to wash and change, if that's all right."

Vince nodded and leaned back against the railings, crossing one ankle over the other.

Jacqui smiled at him and disappeared inside. She shut the door, quietly locking it behind her.

Liam's pack sat on the floor when he'd left it.

She rummaged through it. His passport, wallet and plane ticket were still in it. Her stomach twisted and she knew without a doubt that Vince was lying. That just confirmed her worst fears. There was no way he would go out and leave it behind. Even if he was following a lead of some kind, which is what she'd hoped for in the depths of her heart. Jacqui pulled out the documents and wallet.

Lord God, look after Liam. Something must have happened to him. Looking at wildlife is the last thing I want to do, but I have no choice. Keep him safe until I get back. Let him just have wandered somewhere, or simply have forgotten his ID and money when he went out. Keep watch over him, Lord…thank You…

Jacqui searched through his bag for his phone. It was gone. Would he have taken it with him when they went out earlier? Maybe he put it somewhere else, but where? She glanced around the room and tried all the drawers. Nothing. Then she lifted the pillows. There it was. She slid it into her pocket. Grabbing his camera, she slipped quietly through the connecting door and dropped everything onto her bed. She picked up her pack and put it on the bed as well.

From the bottom of her suitcase, she pulled the concealed body wallet she'd picked up in one of the airport shops at Heathrow. Shoving all Liam's IDs into it, Jacqui strapped it around her waist under a clean shirt. She shouldered the pack and went back the way she'd come.

She stepped out into the sunlight and shut the door. Pulling her shades back over her eyes she gave Vince what she hoped was a convincing smile. "Let's go on a lion hunt."

Vince took tight hold of her hand before she could change her mind, his long strides forcing her to walk fast to keep up.

****

Four hours later, Jacqui threw her sun hat and shades on her bed and scrunched her fists into the small of her back. The lions were amazing, and well worth the trip, but the bumpy ride had played havoc with her muscles.

Liam still wasn't back. One good thing about having to go in and out of 'his room' meant she knew he wasn't there.

Her worry grew. "Where are you, Liam?"

She lay on the bed and closed her eyes, wishing the mattress was firmer. She sighed. Vince had listened to and then dismissed every single one of her ideas for the compound. Whatever he was doing here, wasn't an orphanage. He wanted no playgrounds or covered areas or roses or any planted areas at all. What he needed was a builder not a landscaper. The link had to be to the mining rights, but what could be worth destroying a mission for?

And what did he want her here for? Not to work, obviously. Was this, as she feared all along, just a ploy to get her back?

She had forgotten what being around Vince was like. How he railroaded people into agreeing with him. And so touchy-feely…he insisted on holding her hand, stroking her hair, setting every nerve on edge with fear as he did so.

Liam, by comparison was the total opposite—easy going and unassuming. His touch set her aflame.

Pulling open her pack, she pulled out her passport, ID and plane ticket. She added them to the concealed bag along with Liam's. Just in case Vince decided to hold onto them for safe keeping. Without them she couldn't leave. Something told her that was exactly what Vince had in mind for them both. Any lingering doubts she may have had about Vince's innocence in whatever was going on had now vanished. She prayed the cook got the message out and that help was on the way. Because she was so far out of her depth she was drowning.

Why she thought she could do this, she had no idea. Because she couldn't. It was way bigger than both of them, only Liam wasn't here.

She grabbed her towel and wash stuff. She needed a shower. Being that close to Vince made her skin crawl. Making sure she left by the correct door, Jacqui headed across to the showers. By the time she got there, she was limping.

Her shoe had been beyond uncomfortable since before lunch. Locking the shower stall door, she leaned against it and pulled off her shoe. A piece of paper fell out onto the tiled floor. Bending down, Jacqui picked it up and unfolded it. No wonder her shoe hurt. She frowned at it. Liam's handwriting, but how did it get in her shoe? She looked at the note. One word.

Liberaté.

Jacqui could see Liam under the desk, his fingers touching her foot. He must have slid the note in then. She looked back at it. What did *liberaté* mean?

Showering quickly before the hot water ran out, she dried off and dressed. This time she slid the note into her bra—the safest place she could think of. Then she headed back to the rooms. Both were in darkness. She'd hoped he'd be back by now.

Going inside, even in the failing light, she could see that both rooms were unoccupied.

Maybe he's back and gone to dinner without you.

But even as she thought it, she knew it sounded

hollow. Something was wrong. Glancing around, her stomach plummeted as she realized that his pack was gone. She ran into the other room. Her pack was on the bed where she'd left it, but her Bible was lying next to it, rather than inside it.

The bad feeling she'd had since lunch grew. Why had they taken Liam's pack? Who'd gone through her stuff? Why? She'd only been gone a few minutes. Bile rose in her throat and she swallowed hard. She headed across the compound to the dining hut. She'd ask Vince outright where Liam had gone.

Vince waved as she came into the room. "Jacqui, over here."

Jacqui crossed over to him, her eyes searching the room. "Where's Liam? I can't find him anywhere. You said he'd be back by dark."

"He had to leave. There was a family crisis back in London while we were out. Terry offered him use of the company jet, but he insisted on taking a commercial flight, so I pulled a few strings and got him on the last flight tonight. He was sorry he didn't have time to speak with you before he left, but there wasn't time. He said to tell you bye, and he'll see you when you get back."

Jacqui's fear bloomed large. *God, I'm alone, they've taken Liam...please help me...*

She schooled her features to remain calm. That was a bare faced lie as Liam couldn't leave the country without his passport, and she had that, but now wasn't the time to call him on it. Nor on the fact that her things had been gone through. The less he knew of her plans the better. "Oh. It's not like him to leave without saying goodbye. I needed to speak to him as well. Maybe I can give him a call tomorrow or something."

"Perhaps you'll join me tonight instead. As I said there is something we need to discuss." He grabbed her hand. "Like why you and Liam changed rooms for starters?"

"Oh, yeah, ummm Liam figured with me being the only woman on the compound and all, it would be safer if no one knew where I was sleeping. I mean you wouldn't want one of your men deciding to pay me a midnight visit now, would you?"

"A sensible precaution. Remind me to thank him."

"Yeah, all right, I will. I'll go get something to eat."

Eating with Vince was the last thing she wanted, but she needed to eat, and she didn't wish to arouse his suspicions. Jacqui crossed to the counter and glanced over the selections. Dennis wasn't behind the counter and she glanced up at the server. "Is Dennis around? He promised me chicken tonight."

"Dennis fly home. His mother very, very sick."

"Oh." Jacqui kept her face blank. She really was alone now. There was no way Dennis would leave, not after she told him Liam had gone missing.

"He no have time to make memsahib chicken. We very sorry. Perhaps tomorrow."

"That would be great. Thank you." Deciding on the rice, she picked up a bowl and spoon. She would search for Liam after dinner and get a message to his brother *if* she could get a signal on the phone. If not, there was bound to be a radio somewhere she could use. Liam had to be somewhere, but she had to get word out in case she vanished, too.

Taking the food back to the table, she sat down, eating quietly. She didn't have much of an appetite, but had to eat to keep her strength up. *Lord God, keep him safe wherever he is. Keep Dennis safe. Keep me safe. Let me get a message out before it's too late.*

Vince looked at her. "You're not worried about Liam, are you? We don't need him. He'll get home fine."

"I know he will." *And I need Liam, even if you don't.*

"Have you made a decision? Will you be able to work on what I want?"

She took a deep breath. "I should be able to. It's not quite what I envisioned when you said partners, but..."

Vince's hand closed over hers and Jacqui slowly raised her gaze to meet his.

"I want you as more than a partner, Jac hon. It's all arranged. Sunset tomorrow...you and me..."

"What are you talking about?" she asked hoping her gut instinct was wrong. Surely he didn't mean what she was afraid he did?

Vince reached into his pocket and pulled out a ring. "I want you as my wife. Just think of all we could accomplish."

Jacqui swallowed hard, her stomach threatening to eject her dinner all over the table.

"Well? I expected more of a reaction than that."

"I—I'm sorry. I'm just really tried. It's been a long day. I might go and work on those plans you wanted, while the ideas are fresh in my mind."

Vince's grip tightened. "I've just proposed marriage and you're going to work? I hoped we could spend the evening together, planning..."

"I need time to think and pray about it, Vince. I can't give you a decision right now." She looked at him. "You owe me that at least. Especially if you love me. Now let go and let me get up, please."

"Very well. I want an answer in the morning. The

ceremony is arranged for sunset."

"I see." Would she get no input in that either? Not that she had any intention of marrying him. By sunset tomorrow she'd be as far away as she could. She pushed up and nodded. "Goodnight."

Jacqui left the dining hut swiftly and went back to the rooms.

There was still no sign of Liam. But she didn't expect there to be. Not now. Vince had put Liam well and truly out of the picture. She didn't know where he was, but she knew for sure he wasn't on a plane to London.

She pulled the phone from her bag and turned it on. No signal.

Just a little help, please?

She put the phone onto vibrate and slid it into her pocket. Jacqui grabbed the flashlight from her bag and slid it into her other pocket. There must be a hill or an open area where she could get a signal on the phone. This wasn't the safest thing to do, but what choice did she have?

The man she loved was out there somewhere, probably hurt, possibly more, but she wasn't going to even think that. *Lord, protect him wherever he is. Keep him safe. Let me find him or get a message to his brother or both. All that matters is finding him safe.*

She grabbed her jacket and slid into it, making sure her notepad and pencil were in the top pocket. Jacqui crept down the verandah and outside the building. A row of lights lit the way along the path to the dining hut and the latrines. Following the path, she reached the latrines then branched off behind them. She pulled the phone from her pocket and glanced at it. A glimmer of a signal, one bar. Maybe if she went further along the path the signal would improve.

She walked a bit further, praying hard with every step. Two bars. Would that be enough? She had no choice but to risk it. Squinting at the phone, she scrolled through the list of contacts, hoping he listed Patrick under P and not under a nickname. There were two listed. Patrick home and Patrick mobile. Unsure of the time difference, she dialed the mobile number.

Please, let him be there.

The phone rang and rang. As she was about to hang up, a voice answered. "The lion and the unicorn were fighting for the crown."

What? Totally confused she looked aghast at the phone. That was the last thing she expected. "I'm sorry?"

"The lion and the unicorn were fighting for the crown."

"Is this Patrick?"

"Who is this?"

Jacqui panicked. "It's Jacqui. Umm…" *What's my code name? It was something Biblical, they both were and they were a matching pair. Oh think, woman. Jezebel, Esther, Rachel, Deborah…Delilah. That was it.* "It's Delilah. I'm using Samson's phone."

"I explicitly told him no contact. Do you have the correct code? The lion and the unicorn were fighting for the crown."

What was the next line? "The lion beat the unicorn twice around the town."

"I'm sorry. That's not it."

"Please, it's important. Samson's missing, and so's Den…Rhubarb—" The line went dead. Tears filled her eyes. Now what did she do?

19

Liam opened his eyes as water splashed into his face, dripping down his chest. Every part of his body hurt. A figure stood over him, the nauseating smell of sweat and stale alcohol on his breath, making Liam gag.

"So you're awake. Good. Perhaps you'll answer some questions for me."

Terry's back.

Liam experimentally moved his jaw. It was swollen and sore from the previous beating he'd received.

Oh, Lord, help me here. Don't let me give anything away and above all keep Jacqui safe. She's out there with Vince and she's alone. I know a little of what he's capable of but—

An eye watering punch shoved his head to one side, cutting off his prayer. Liam gasped as pain skyrocketed through his neck and shoulders. With his hands firmly tied behind his back, holding him prisoner on the chair, there was no way he could retaliate.

"I asked you a question."

"I didn't hear you. I'm sorry. Perhaps you could repeat it."

"Where did you meet the new cook, Dennis? Are you plotting something together?"

"Never met him before today," Liam replied

truthfully. "And hardly exchanged two words with him."

Another punch sent his head flying the other way. "Liar."

"Why would I lie?"

"You and Miss Dorne spoke to him, and he was found in the radio room sending a coded signal. He refused to say anything. He died screaming. Exactly the same way that you will."

"Don't be so sure."

"Perhaps I should ask Miss Dorne these questions. Or tell Vince she's betrayed him. He won't like that."

"She hasn't betrayed him. She doesn't know anything about anything. She came out here because Vince asked her to. I didn't want to come."

"Too many bad memories, maybe? Are you not enjoying being back where you wife died?"

"What do you think? Tell me, what does Vince want the land for? It looks like he's got a fairly impressive military style operation set up here. Having a bunch of kids in an orphanage would cramp his style."

"Shut up!" Another swift blow sent his senses reeling. Stars floated in front of his eyes, followed by a hard punch to his stomach which drove the air from his lungs. Unable to even bend double, Liam sat there, gasping for breath. *Forgive him, Lord...*

Terry moved back into his field of vision holding what looked like jump leads for a car attached to a battery pack. "Then let me ask again only this time I want the truth."

"I told you the truth."

"I was hoping you'd say that." Terry touched the two metal clips together and the air sparked blue with electricity.

Liam swallowed hard. *Lord, God, help me.*

Terry moved over to him. "Let's see if I can change your mind."

Liam closed his eyes. No matter what happened he'd remain quiet. He wasn't going to betray Jacqui or Patrick. He focused his attention on the Lord, starting to sing 'Jesus, lover of my soul' in his mind. He could do this, he had to, and if he were to die here, then he'd leave it up to God to save Jacqui.

****

Jacqui stood there, the dead phone in her hand. How could Patrick cut her off? Didn't he care about his brother at all? It wasn't her fault she didn't know what the code was? There was no one else she could call. She shook her head. Of course there was. Closing her eyes, she prayed hard. Then rubbing away the tears, she took a deep breath.

With God's help, she could do this. The man she loved depended on her, on them, and she wasn't going to let him down.

Now think. Liam has to be here somewhere. You know he hasn't left the country. Start by searching the outbuildings.

Jacqui started walking back towards the compound. She had taken three steps when the phone in her hand vibrated. It didn't recognize the number, but she answered anyway. "Hello?"

"Jacqui, this is Patrick. This is a secure line this time, so the number won't be traced. Can you talk?"

She swung around and started pacing again, looking as if she were working. "Yeah."

"Where's Liam?"

"I don't know. We got separated. Vince wanted to talk to me alone, so he dragged me off, despite Liam's objections. I assumed Liam was going to snoop a bit, but I haven't seen him since. First Vince said Liam had gone shopping, but he didn't take his wallet or any ID. So I put them with mine to keep them safe. Then just now Vince said Liam had flown home because of a family emergency, but his bag is still here, or at least it was, and I know he didn't take a commercial flight like Vince said as I have Liam's passport. But in the three minutes I was in the shower, his bag has gone and mine was broken into and—"

"Slow down, you're babbling and I can't understand you. Leave out the circumstances for now and stick to Liam. When did you last see him?" Patrick's no nonsense tone cut her off.

"About five hours ago. He was finding it really hard, being back here. When he didn't show for dinner...I thought you should know."

"Why didn't you send a message via the other channel?"

"I did...well at lunch I mentioned the chicken dish to the cook, but then Vince appeared so I made a random comment about Liam having abandoned me figuring you'd get the message."

"I haven't heard anything since yesterday when you arrived. Where's Dennis now?"

"According to the server at dinner, he went home because his mother was sick."

"I see." Patrick's voice tightened. "I'll get things rolling from this end. Had either of you found anything yet?"

"Vince wants to marry me, and it's definitely not

an orphanage he wants built out here. Other than that...oh, hang on—Liam was hiding under Vince's desk and stuck a note in my shoe. It said Liberaté."

"Liberaté? Are you sure?"

"Yes."

"Spell it for me?"

"L-i-b-e-r-a-t-e. It has one of those slant things over the e. A forward slash one, I think."

"OK, thanks. Was there anything else on the note?"

"No. Just the one word. Liberaté. I have no idea what it means, but Liam must have thought it was important."

"I'll look into it and get back to you. I need you to do something for me."

"What's that? Other than don't marry Vince." She laughed nervously. "You need to get me out of here before sunset tomorrow. Or I need to get myself out."

"Well, yeah. Keep your head down. Don't do anything to arouse any more suspicion. And don't call me again. I'll call you."

The line went dead. Jacqui closed the phone and slid it into her pocket. She wasn't expecting to hear back from Patrick. It was up to her to find Liam and get them out of here. First port of call was the outbuildings on the edge of the compound.

She walked back towards them, waving at the guards. She smiled as they waved back. As she walked, Jacqui pulled out a notebook and counted aloud, as if she were measuring the distance. Every so often she'd scribble the numbers down on the paper. She shone the flashlight at the door on the first outbuilding. They were single story, one room buildings, which she expected were storage sheds, and all were in complete darkness.

Pushing the door open, Jacqui moved the torch around. Empty. One down, six to go. She moved on to the next, feeling more confident in her ability to do this. If this took all night, so be it. Ten minutes later, she had six buildings crossed off her list, and she moved onto the next row.

"Memsahib?" Jacqui closed her eyes at the intrusive voice and turned around to see Simeon running across to her. "Memsahib…"

Forcing a smile to rival his, Jacqui moved over to him. "Yes?"

"Sahib Devlin, he have need of you now. Urgent."

"I'm busy. It will have to wait."

"No, can not wait. He say you come now. Very, very important you come now."

"Then lead on." Jacqui followed Simeon across the compound, tuning out his chatter. What did Vince want that was so important? It wasn't news of Liam — that much she was sure of. Even if Vince had used a private plane to fly Liam home, he wouldn't get far without the passport sitting in the pouch wrapped around her stomach.

Vince stood in his office.

"What is it?"

Vince turned and smiled, holding out a glass of wine to her. "I wanted to see you."

"And I'm trying to work."

"It's late, sweetheart, and I want to see this ring on your finger tonight. You've had plenty of time to consider my proposal, and I'm sure you're in agreement with me, that is really is for the best. For everyone."

"What do you mean by *everyone*?"

Vince held her gaze. "It would be a terrible shame if Liam's flight met with an accident or he was detained by customs for importing something illegal. Wouldn't it?"

Chills ran down her spine. "OK," she whispered.

"I didn't hear you. Will you marry me?"

"Yes." The words were torn from her soul, ripping the heart from her. She'd do it to save Liam. Her heart belonged to the tall, Irish gentleman who'd thrown flowers over her laptop. She cleared her throat. "Yes, Vince. I'll marry you."

He slid the ring onto her finger. "There, was that so bad?"

Jacqui stood still and closed her eyes, turning her head at the last moment as he leaned in for a kiss, his lips brushing her cheek. She tried not to shudder, her whole being repulsed by his touch.

Vince's fingers slid under her chin, tilting her face back towards him. "What were you doing by the storage units?" The glint in his eyes belied the silky voice and smile on his lips.

"Measuring." She held his gaze, refusing to be intimidated by him. Not anymore.

"I don't believe you."

Jacqui pulled out her notebook and thrust it at him, grateful for the forethought to have taken notes. "Here, check it then."

His fingers brushed hers as he took it. "Why measure in the dark when you can't see what you're doing?" He studied the book. "And this is a mess. It looks like random numbers. How can you make any sense of it?"

Jacqui sighed. "It's called pacing the area out. It makes perfect sense if you know what you're doing—

which I do." She took the book back. "Now, if you don't mind, I want to do the rest of that side before it gets any later."

Vine's hand caught tight hold of her wrist. "Actually, I do mind. You haven't touched your wine."

"I don't drink. You should know that."

"Tonight you will." His tone left her in no doubt that it wasn't an option, with its veiled threat. "Here."

Jacqui took the glass he offered, her fingers white against it.

"To us. May we live long and prosper."

"Deuteronomy chapter five, verse thirty three," she told him, reluctantly chinking her glass against his. She forced herself to drink, wrinkling her nose and trying not to gag.

"Interesting." He sat in his chair, pulling her down onto his lap. "One drink, a cuddle and you can go."

Jacqui closed her eyes as the smell of alcohol washed over her. It was clear this wasn't his first of the night. She stiffened as his fingers caressed her arm and his lips pressed into her hair. *Now what? I don't want to anger him, who knows what he'd do, but I can't do this. I won't do this.*

The phone rang. Vince picked it up. "Devlin. Yeah I'm in the middle of something…" He straightened and pushed Jacqui off his lap. "What? When did that happen?" He pulled the pad towards him. "Well of course I do."

Jacqui set the glass down and made a quick exit while he was distracted. *Thank you, Lord.* She headed back across to the storage sheds, and reached the ones she hadn't already checked. She found each one empty and unlocked. The final one contained a pile of crates.

As tempting as it was to look inside them, Jacqui

knew she didn't have time. She had to find Liam, assuming he was still here, before it got light. Leaving the building, she slowly made her way through the ruins to a large building that had caught her attention that morning. Half destroyed by the fire, it had a brand new door on it. Hefting the flashlight in her right hand, she tried the door.

It was locked. Why put a new door on a ruin if not to keep something safe, or to stop someone getting in?

Or out came the voice inside her. *Perhaps Liam is in there.*

She reached up and pulled a hairpin from her hair. This couldn't be that hard. She'd seen it on the TV loads of times and been shown how to jimmy a lock during the few days training she'd been given.

She slid the grip into the lock and jiggled it. She reinserted the hairpin, and this time there was a faint click. Trying the handle again, she allowed herself a small smile when it moved. She pushed the door open, gritting her teeth as it creaked and shone the flashlight around the room. She caught her breath as a pair of eyes reflected at her.

*****

Liam still had the same splitting headache and nausea in his gut he'd woken with several hours ago, when he realized he was tied to a chair in the dark. Now the pain was infinitely worse. He assumed he had burn marks where Terry had attached the electrodes. Terry had kept going until he passed out.

He tried moving his hands, but Terry knew how to tie knots, as his hands and feet wouldn't move, despite his wrists being slick with blood. His gaze followed the creaking door as it swung open. His stomach plummeted, and a sickening fear filled him. Maybe Terry was coming back to finish the job. This time adding the second bucket of water he'd threatened. *Let it be swift. Just please get Jacqui away from here unharmed.*

A light shone in his face, blinding him. Liam wished he could fling a hand over his eyes to protect them instead he turned his head to one side. His breathing sped up and his heart pounded. He tensed automatically, waiting for the blow or gunshot that would send him to heaven. Or a drenching in cold water followed by the worse kind of pain he'd ever known.

"Liam?"

He didn't react. It couldn't be her. He sat still trying to work out why she was here. Only when the voice repeated his name and footsteps crossed the room, did he open his eyes. He squinted against the light. "Jacqui?"

"Yes." Her voice was a gasp, and her arms folded around him, her lips seeking his in sheer desperation.

He kissed Jacqui back, but her hug hurt, and he stiffened, stifling the gasp of pain. He didn't want to worry her.

Jacqui pulled back, concern in her voice and eyes. "Liam, what's wrong? Did I hurt you?"

"No, my love, you didn't. I'm just stiff. Can you untie me, please? Then I can hug you back."

"Of course." Jacqui moved behind him.

He flexed his hands as she undid the knots, wondering if he were dreaming again. Pain and pins and needles shot through them as the blood circulated. He closed his eyes, breathing deeply. *Just deal with it.* Once his feet were free, she pulled him upright.

Liam staggered, his knees and legs too weak to support him.

"Take it easy, big fella." Jacqui steadied him. "All right?"

He nodded and wrapped his arms around her, kissing her deeply.

Her hands curled around his back, pulling his battered body against her soft, yielding one.

After a minute, Jacqui broke off, her breath coming in soft gasps. "We have to go, Liam."

"I know, the question is where to and how. We won't get out of here easily. Vince has a thick file on me in his office. He knows who I am, and that I know what he's up to here. I'm a threat to him. He's already killed Dennis and I'm next."

"Oh, ye of little faith. God won't leave us here. We'll go back to your room. It's the last place they'll look. I'll contact Patrick again."

"You rang Patrick? But you don't know the code."

Jacqui's laugh was short. "Yeah, been there, done that and won the dunce's cap for messing it up. But I gave him the message from the note you slid into my shoe. I wondered why they were so uncomfortable."

"You're pretty resourceful for a gardener."

He loved the way her eyes sparkled. "No more so than you are, Mr. English Teacher."

He pulled her close and kissed her again. He didn't think he'd ever see her again, and now he never intended to let her go.

Her fingers moved through his hair, and he stiffened, letting out an involuntary cry of pain as they found the lump on the back of his head.

She pulled back, looking at her blood covered fingers. "You're bleeding."

"That's the least of my injuries. We need to get out of here. Maybe we can steal a truck. If I hide in the back and you drive. You could say you're going to pick up supplies for the work you're doing." He took her hand and led her to the door.

"Oh, can we check something first? I found some crates."

"Sure, show me. We'll need to be very quick, though."

The sun was rising, and a pale light flooded the room as he peeked outside. Taking firm hold of her hand, they made their way back to the outbuildings Jacqui checked earlier. She pushed open the door and showed him the crates. Liam took a couple of photos on the pen camera and was about to open one when he heard shouting. "They've worked it out. We need to get out of here, now."

Liam was about to put the pen away when Jacqui shook her head. "What?" he asked.

"Give it to me."

Confused, he nevertheless did as she asked, his confusion giving way to a wide grin as she tucked it inside her shirt. "What *are* you doing?"

Jacqui winked. "It's now perfectly safe along with the note. No one would dare look there for it. And if they do, I'm depending on you to protect a lady's honor."

Liam just hoped she was right, but if she wasn't... "I'd die to protect your honor, Miss Jacqui."

"Hopefully that won't be necessary, but it's a lovely offer."

He gave her a lopsided grin. "All right, then let's go." He took her hand and moved towards the door. He pushed it open and glanced around. "All right.

Maybe we'll manage to get out..."

He broke off as something hard hit his back, making him cry out involuntarily as more pain ripped him in two. "Or maybe we won't."

"Turn around. Very slowly and put your hands up."

Liam turned, moving in front of Jacqui, shielding her with his body.

Two armed men stood in front of them—Terry and Simeon. Terry sneered. "Some people don't know when to give in." He reached out, punching Liam hard, sending him staggering away from Jacqui and onto the ground.

Liam struggled upright, desperate to protect Jacqui. "Leave her—" He broke off as Terry shoved his gun into Jacqui's side, the fingers of his other hand digging into her arm.

"I wouldn't do that if I were you." Terry's voice was cold.

She looked at him, her eyes wide with fear.

"Or you'll what?" Liam asked.

"Vince wants her alive. He'll accept hurt."

Liam struggled as Simeon grabbed hold of him. "You won't get away with this."

Terry laughed. "I think you'll find we already have. Vince wants to see you both. Now."

20

Jacqui walked as slowly as she could. Terry led her to where Vince waited. They left the safety of the compound, walking the hundred paces or so down a well-worn path. She could hear water running and guessed it was the river. Under normal circumstances, she'd have been impressed with the beauty of the wide blue water, but not today. She glared at Vince. "What do you want?"

Vince stood by the river, gazing out over it. He turned ice cold eyes on her. "I want you. I thought I made that abundantly clear. But you insisted on bringing this Irish riff raff with you."

She shook her head, feeling sick. "You set this whole thing up to get me back?"

"Not just that. You're the icing on the cake. With you in charge here, no one will question what Terry and I are doing. There's a huge diamond mine worth millions under this place. Your work here will be the cover to get them out. While you stand at my side as my wife."

"Why not do it legally? You own the land and the mining rights." Her brows creased. "Wait a minute. Is that why you slaughtered everyone here? Money?"

"We tried negotiating with them, but they wouldn't listen."

"But you own the land. You could just have terminated their contract," she insisted.

"It's not just the land, is it?" Liam interjected. "You're using the money to fund Liberaté."

Vince's eyes narrowed and his whole body exuded hatred and anger. "How do you know about Liberaté?"

"I have my sources—you should take better care of your files." He looked at Jacqui. "He's funding a revolution. You're looking at the man who would be potentate or despot of this region, and then the entire country, eventually. That's why he blew up the restaurant and tried to assassinate the vice president."

"What?" She looked at Vince. "You're seriously trying to lead a rebellion here?"

"It's not a rebellion. It's giving these people the freedom they crave. And yes I am funding it. The mission was in the way. This will make the perfect base of operations to train the men."

Liam shook off Simeon's grip and took a step towards Vince, his eyes narrowing. "You killed my wife and the others because we were *in the way*?"

"They were casualties of war. A terrorist attack that everyone, apart from you, has long since forgotten. You'll die here, just like your wife did and be reunited with her. A bittersweet reunion, but nonetheless a touching one." He jerked his head at Terry and Simeon.

The two men grabbed his arms and dragged him to the river's edge.

"Let go of me."

"Vince, please, don't."

Vince grabbed hold of Jacqui, pulling her towards him. "Vince, please, don't," he mimicked. "Don't what?" He drew her closer. "I can do whatever I like, princess. Your boyfriend is going to meet a tragic end.

So sad, but he should never have gone swimming in a crocodile infested river in the first place. Especially after both you and I warned him and begged him not to. He just couldn't stand the idea that you returned to your old lover and chose him instead. We'll marry tonight as planned, and live happily ever after."

She closed her eyes and turned her face away as he tried to kiss her. "You're sick."

Vince laughed. "It's all arranged. You and I marry at sunset, and finally you are mine and can put me off no longer. There is nothing you can do to stop it. I win."

She struggled. "Want to bet? Liam-m-m-m-m-m-m."

****

At the sound of her desperate cry, Liam pulled away from the two men. He used his left leg to knock Terry to the ground. The gun went flying across the earth. Before he could reach it, Terry's hand gripped his ankle and tugged. Liam plunged quickly into the dirt.

The breath whooshed from his lungs as he landed hard, face down in the mud and sand, already sore ribs screaming in protest at yet further damage. He rolled, pushing himself upright, lashing out with his leg again, and aiming for Simeon who landed hard and rolled.

Liam glanced at Jacqui needing to make sure she was safe.

Vince had firm hold of her, despite her struggles.

That brief glimpse cost him dear, as he found himself flying through the air before landing on his back close to the river. He rolled over, trying to escape Simeon's fist as it pounded into him relentlessly. Managing to get a few blows of his own in, he realized he was defending more than anything else.

A splash from the opposite bank caught his attention and he jerked up. The crocodiles had started to take notice of what was going on and one of the bigger ones started swimming across the river. More splashes echoed across the water, each one as loud as a death knell.

Liam struggled only to be floored by a punch which sent him sprawling. Sand and grit filled his mouth and nose, and he choked. As he tried to scramble up, Simeon kicked him. Liam grunted as he landed on his stomach, inhaling yet more sand. A knee landed heavily on Liam's back and a firm grip twisted in his hair before pushing his face under the water.

The pressure in his chest grew, sounds becoming muffled. Darkness began to descend and his movements slowed.

He heard someone calling his name. Jacqui. He had to get to Jacqui.

Not like this. Not while Jacqui's in danger. God, please, help me. If You want me that's fine. I'm willing to die, but not yet. Let me get Jacqui safe first. She's the only thing that matters.

Something brushed against his face, and he jerked, losing more of the air he had left. He struggled and managed to roll clear. He lay on his back, gasping for breath, and then sucked in a short breath of pain as someone kicked him in the ribs. He turned and pushed himself to his hands and knees, twisting as his attacker lunged at him.

Water flew into the air as Simeon misjudged the

leap and fell into the river.

Screams and splashes came as a waiting crocodile launched into a death roll.

Liam stood watching, hands braced on knees, his breath coming in gasps. There was no time to take in the water slowly staining red, before Terry came at him with a right hook which sent him to the ground. Pushing up, he fought back, kicking and spinning.

As he swept out with his right leg, Terry went down, and Liam was grateful Patrick had insisted on martial arts classes for stress relief in the early days after Sally's death.

They drew closer to the river, forcing Liam backwards under the onslaught. He lashed out with his leg again, sending Terry sliding over the bank and into the water.

Terry cried out, looking in fear over his shoulder at the crocodiles busy tearing apart their previous spoils. He tried to reach the shore, but the current pulled him towards the huge river beasts. "Help me. I can't swim." He screamed and went under. His head bobbed up, stark terror in his eyes.

Without a second thought, Liam dived in.

21

"Liam...no!" Jacqui screamed as Liam dived into the blood red water.

The crocodiles turned and headed towards the two men.

"Liam." She turned to Vince. "Do something."

He shook his head.

Jacqui kicked back and up with her foot, making sharp contact with the apex of Vince's thighs, something she wished she'd had the courage to do years ago when he hurt her. As Vince doubled over, she tore free and ran to the river. "Liam..."

Liam grabbed Terry and started swimming to the bank, pulling him as fast as he could. Dropping to her hands and knees, Jacqui leaned out, ready to help pull the men out of the water.

Liam heaved Terry upwards, and Jacqui grabbed his shirt, tugging the unconscious figure to dry land. She glanced up as the crocodiles got closer. "Liam, take my hand."

He grabbed her outstretched hand, and she pulled him clear as the crocodile pounced, missing him by a fraction. He knelt on the ground, water dripping from every part of him, shaking hard, gasping for breath.

Jacqui wrapped her arms around him tightly, not caring she was going to get soaked. "You're an idiot."

Liam's lips brushed hers. "Maybe...but...I wasn't...going to let...him...die." He interspaced his words with small, frantic kisses.

"He almost killed you." Jacqui helped him to his feet.

"No reason to let him die."

A click sounded, and they raised their eyes to see Vince holding himself with one hand and pointing a gun at them with the other. "Unfortunately for you, I don't have the same morals."

Jacqui caught her breath. "Then you have to kill us both, Vince, because if you expect me to keep quiet about all this, you've got another think coming," she said, wondering if her contempt of him was as palpable as it felt.

"If that's what you want."

"It is. I won't marry you. Liam is worth a dozen of you any day." She pulled the ring off and threw it at him. "Here. Even if you paid me, I—" She broke off as Vince slapped her. Her hand flew to her cheek.

"Leave her alone." Liam took a step forward.

Jacqui stayed his hand, lacing her fingers firmly into his, and shook her head. She took a deep breath. "He's not worth it."

Vince waved the gun at her. "Get on your knees."

She shook her head. "I bow to no one except God."

"Drop this religious kick, and marry me, and I'll let you live."

"I will not betray my Lord, or the man I love." Jacqui looked at him intently. "Want me to say it again?"

"One last chance."

"You heard her, Vince. We belong to God first and to each other. There is nothing else that matters. You can kill our bodies, but our souls are safe for eternity."

"So be it." Vince scowled and fired the gun

directly over her head. "I said on your knees. The next shot won't miss."

"No, we won't." Liam pulled Jacqui into his arms, shielding her as much as possible.

"No." Jacqui shook hard, tears pricking her eyes despite herself. Liam's arms tightened around her, and she closed her eyes.

Liam prayed aloud, and Jacqui wanted to, but she didn't know what to say for fear of it sounding trite. "Lord, we come before You, asking for shelter in Your arms…" Liam's voice was a balm to her soul.

"We could have been so good together. Goodbye, princess." The smirk in Vince's voice hung in the air.

There was a gunshot, and she tensed waiting for the pain, which didn't come. Liam didn't fall. Who'd been shot? Had Vince missed at point blank range? Shouts echoed and another shot, followed by a scream of pain.

"Everybody down!" She didn't recognize the voice, but the authority in it resonated almost as loud as the gunfire.

Liam pulled her to the ground, covering her with his body, and she clung to him. She lay motionless, heart pounding, scared witless and praying hard.

After a minute or two the gunfire ceased and a deadly silence covered the whole clearing.

Jacqui didn't move.

Liam's unaccustomed weight was heavy, but she felt safe. As he moved, her whole being was filled with a sense of loss and she whimpered.

"Jacqui? Are you all right?" Liam's voice was calmer than she expected.

"I'm fine." She opened her eyes. "What happened?"

"The cavalry arrived."

She sat up and followed his gaze. Patrick and a team of flak-jacketed agents, along with several uniformed officers, swarmed the area.

Vince lay face down on the ground, his hands pulled behind him in cuffs. He writhed and cursed everyone he could see.

Terry lay still, also in cuffs.

"Oh…" Jacqui turned to Liam, holding him tightly, allowing the tears to fall now that it was all over.

Liam ran his hands over her back, his soft lips trailing kisses through her hair. "It's all right," he whispered. Then he prayed quietly, thanking God for delivering them.

Patrick crossed over to them. "Hey, sorry it took so long."

Liam stood and helped Jacqui to her feet. He held out a hand to his brother. "Not a moment too soon. I'm glad you got here." He paused. "How did you get here so fast? If Jacqui rang you last night then…"

Patrick raised an eyebrow. "Do you really think I'd send you in without any kind of backup? I've been in the next village, but had to wait for a team from Endarra before I could get here."

Jacqui released Liam and watched the two men embrace. Someone wrapped a blanket around her shoulders, and she hugged it. She moved to one side, adding her prayers to what Liam had already said, thanking God for saving them. Liam's arms came around her.

"Are you sure you're all right, love?"

She leaned against the strong chest, closing her eyes. "I'm all right, Liam. I just want to go home."

Patrick's voice came from her left, and she opened her eyes as he touched her arm. "You can go home as soon as you've both been debriefed. Again, I apologize for being rude on the phone. The line wasn't secure, and you didn't have the code word."

"It's fine. Just out of interest, what was it as it wasn't the next line of the rhyme?"

He grinned and turned at Liam. "The lion and the unicorn were fighting for the crown."

Liam wrung the water from the edge of his shirt. "Seven for a secret, never to be told."

"Well, that makes perfect sense. How's a girl meant to guess that?" Jacqui complained. "Men."

Liam raised an eyebrow and tilted his head. "And what's wrong with men?"

She kept her face straight, despite wanting to grin at him. "Can't live with them, can't kill them, just have to kiss them."

"I can go along with that." He smiled and kissed her.

Jacqui closed her eyes, and parted her lips, returning the kiss with as much passion, not caring he was kissing her in front of his brother and several armed police officers. All that mattered was that she was here with Liam and that God had protected them through this, just as she asked.

22

By the time they reached Headley Cross after a long flight and a ninety minute train journey, the sky was grey and threatening rain. So different from the clear blue African skies they left behind.

Patrick offered to have them driven home from the airport, but Jacqui refused. She wanted stability and some things that were quintessentially British—a train, long queues, and coffee from the railway buffet cars that neither resembled nor tasted anything like coffee.

The only thing she'd let Patrick do was deal with the luggage, which he promised to have delivered to their respective houses that evening.

Liam hugged her close. "Want to go straight home?"

She shook her head as she hugged him back. "No. Can we do something normal first?"

"Like what?"

"I want to go shopping. Hit the town center."

"What's the town center done to deserve being hit?"

Jacqui snorted and playfully tugged on his arm. "Not literally. I need milk and bread and silly things like that."

"We can do that. Especially as I need those, too. Along with some cereal or something for breakfast in the morning. And a ready meal for dinner."

"Then I want to go play pooh sticks. In a river that

doesn't have crocodiles in it. At least I don't think it has." She winked at him. "You want to swim in it to find out?"

"I'll take a rain check on that one. Thanks for the thought."

They visited the refreshingly boring supermarket where the most exciting thing that happened was Liam insisting on paying. He promised Jacqui she could return the favor by cooking him dinner later in the week, and then ran ahead to open the door for her. "There you go, my love."

"Thank you." She made her way through it.

"You're welcome."

"So where next?" She tugged up her collar. "Ugh, it's raining. Now I know I'm back in England."

"Hey, I thought you wanted boring and normal and British. You can't get more normal in England than rain."

"True. And it's your fault." She playfully nudged his arm.

He rubbed it and nudged her back. "How'd you work that one out?"

"You said you'd take a rain check. Well check it out, it's raining."

Liam roared with laughter. "OK, OK, I'll take the blame for the rain. However, the rain isn't going to be a problem." Liam pulled an umbrella from the bag and held it over her as they walked down the street.

"You're being terribly gallant, Liam. Would you lay your coat over puddles, too, so my feet don't get wet?"

"No. I'll carry you over them."

Jacqui glanced at him and then down at the bag in her hand. "You're not going to offer to carry the shopping as well?"

"How am I meant to open doors, hold umbrellas, and carry you over puddles if my hands are full of bags?"

She shook her head. "Men."

Liam grinned and kissed her. "I know. You can't live with them, can't kill them..."

"Just have to kiss them," Jacqui finished. The rain thudded against the umbrella, but she ignored it, losing herself in the company of the man walking next to her. So much had changed, but so much had stayed the same.

As they reached the bridge, the rain stopped. Jacqui grabbed a couple of sticks and handed one to Liam. She stood still, the wind blowing her hair as she leaned over the edge. "One, two, three." The sticks fell and she ran to the other side, cheering as her stick won.

"Well done."

"Thank you." She leaned on the barrier, staring down at the water.

Liam stood behind her, wrapping his arms around her. "Penny for them."

Jacqui smiled. "Thinking how pretty it is."

"Like you."

"Flattery will get you everywhere, Mr. Page."

"That's what I'm hoping, Miss Dorne. Especially since my love is even prettier than sunsets."

She smiled and wrapped her arms over his. "Not as handsome as mine is."

She leaned against him, as the sun peeped through the clouds and touched the water, sending an orange glow across it.

"Jacqui, I have something I want to ask you."

She twisted her head over her shoulder at him,

gazing into his eyes. The light set them afire and made them more gorgeous than ever. "What's that?"

Liam looked at her seriously. "When are you ever going to let me win at pooh sticks?"

"Never."

"All right…guess I can live with that. On one condition, though."

"Uh oh. What's the condition?"

He turned her to face him. "I love you, Jacqui. I have since the moment I met you. That moment you said you'd rather die than be without me, made me realize how much I loved you and that you loved me the same way. Would you do me the honor of becoming my wife?"

Jacqui held his gaze for a moment. "Liam, I…"

He smiled. "I love you. I came so close to losing you, and I don't want that. I don't want to spend another day without you in my life. I've put the past to rest, we both have, and I'm convinced the path ahead that God wants us to travel is together."

Tears sparkled in her eyes. "Yes…yes, I'll marry you."

He hugged her tightly, his arms folding around her back. "I love you."

Jacqui looked up into the eyes of man she had been willing to die for, rather than betray. Joy bubbled up and overflowed. "I love you, too."

Liam leaned down and kissed her, showing her how much he loved her in a way words couldn't express.

She tried to contain the blush spreading over her cheeks and the way her knees weakened and her legs didn't want to hold her up anymore.

Liam adjusted his grip to keep her upright.

Jacqui held him tightly, stars dancing around her. She parted her lips, allowing him to deepen the kiss, kissing him until they both stood breathless, foreheads touching, arms and fingers entwined. She stifled a yawn, not wanting to spoil the moment.

He ran a finger down her face, sending sparks of electricity pouring through her. "Can you stay awake long enough for a rematch before I take you home?"

Jacqui nodded. "Just don't expect me to let you win."

Liam smiled and leaned down picking up two sticks. "We'll see. One more game, then home."

"That sounds good. Homeward bound."

Liam grinned as he counted to three and the sticks fell. "Heavenward bound, actually." He ran to the other side. He had won the woman he loved, salvation from a God who loved him and as the sticks passed underneath them, his hand punched the air. "Finally. Yes!"

Thank you for purchasing this White Rose Publishing title. For other inspirational stories, please visit our online bookstore at www.pelicanbookgroup.com.

For questions or more information, contact us at titleadmin@pelicanbookgroup.com.

White Rose Publishing
Where Faith is the Cornerstone of Love™
www.WhiteRosePublishing.com
an imprint of Pelican Ventures Book Group
www.PelicanBookGroup.com

May God's glory shine through
this inspirational work of fiction.

AMDG